PRAISE FOR *THE L*

"Young journalist Violet Maris tells a daring lie that launches her on a collision course with the truth about herself. 'You just can't trust a writer,' Violet says. Trust Diane Wald to write a beautifully unsparing, rollickingly funny, tender story about fact and fiction, love and art, set in the creative hub of 1980s Provincetown. A great read you won't want to put down."

—Philip Bennett, former managing editor, *The Washington Post*

"Once I started Diane Wald's *The Bayrose Files* I couldn't put it down. The book is written in first person, so it's easy to get inside the protagonist, Violet's, head. She is quirky, and so real that I fell in love with her from the first page. The author writes beautiful, visual prose, the story moves at the perfect pace to lure you in, and you're sad when it's over. I loved this novel and I'm sure you will, too."

—Leslie A. Rasmussen, author of *After Happily Ever After* and *The Stories We Cannot Tell*

"*The Bayrose Files* is a gem of a book, taking us into the creative and complex world of an art colony, seen through the eyes of an impostor. The characters, story, structure, language, setting, and pacing are brilliant.

The moral lessons are gentle, human foibles forgivable. I devoured it in a single sitting and remain in awe of Diane Wald's imagination."

—Romalyn Tilghman, author of *To the Stars Through Difficulties*

"I gulped down *The Bayrose Files* in one sitting. What starts as a simple story of deception unspools into a tale of grief, love, and complicated regret. In prose that crackles, Diane Wald crafts a marvelous storyteller in Violet Maris. Violet is sharp, endearing, and deeply human. It was a pleasure to follow her every bad decision. Violet—and Wald—kept me guessing until the last page."

—Miriam Gershow, author of *Closer* and *Survival Tips: Stories*

"For Violet Maris, the temperature varies in inanimate objects. This is her guide in The Home, a prestigious artist colony in Provincetown where, as a journalist, she poses as a fiction writer in order to write an exposé. Following the relative heat of things, she navigates the death of a dear friend, a love affair with a board member, and her own deceit. Of course, there is a reckoning, but it is not what she expects, in this metaphysical and gripping story where the pages seem to turn by themselves. What will touch her now?"

—William C. Dell, author of *Home Alone in the Multiverse* and *Time's Hidden Dimension*

"In *The Bayrose Files*, Diane Wald's quirky narrator spins a strange story as oddly poignant as its setting: an artists' community in early '80s Provincetown. The moody, seductive atmosphere of this town and that time offers a fitting backdrop for this tale of betrayal and imposture. Violet Maris, named for the sea, tells a story of shifting currents, fogs of betrayal, emotional shipwreck, and ultimate confession. Wald's story is smart and moving, a search for lost time and a reckoning with ghosts."

—Cynthia Huntington, author of *The Salt House* and *Heavenly Bodies*

"When twenty-six-year-old journalist Violet Maris goes undercover to write an exposé of a budding literary colony in Provincetown, a place with 'no restrictions…on what a person could look like, or be, or even pretend to be,' the story she ends up telling is not at all what she expected. With sympathy and warmth, vividness and keen humor, Diane Wald chronicles Violet's painful, belated coming of age, while bringing to life a raucous, randy, dedicated cast of artists and writers. Long after *The Bayrose Files* ends, you will find Violet living on in your imagination: her ambitions, regrets, losses, and conscience pangs are keenly relatable, as is her journey toward authenticity, accountability, and living up to her heart's potential."

—Karen Holmberg, author of *The Collagist*

"A zippy tale, à la rogue journalism, that hopes to blow the lid off art poseurs and writing colonies, Diane Wald's *The Bayrose Files* instead finds a genuine heart on Cape Cod. As anyone who's ever been to Provincetown knows, there's a certain slant of light, color, atmosphere. Wald's novella captures this brilliantly, especially the sharp clarities of Ptown off season. In a loosely veiled send up of the Fine Arts Work Center, Wald—a former fellow—finds the bona fides in the details: weather, seafood, dank bars, western sunsets at Herring Cove. But there's something more. Episodic, witty, and then unexpectedly moving, it's a story about a would-be writer who's also strangely a thermopath, a 'she who senses when things get hot.' Wald's Violet Maris knows things when she touches them. *The Bayrose Files* captures endings, beginnings, love, loss, shame—all the vicissitudes that beset any of us trying to be authentic. Read *The Bayrose Files* and smell the brine."

—Matthew Cooperman, author of *Wonder About The*

"In spare and evocative prose, *The Bayrose Files* chronicles the coming-of-age of a misguided young journalist who goes under false pretenses to an artists' residency in off-season 1980s Provincetown. Diane Wald draws a compelling portrait of a complicated young woman forced to grapple with the cost of her ambition and the inevitability of regret. I thoroughly enjoyed this refreshingly unsentimental novel."

—Karen Dukess, author of *The Last Book Party*

THE BAYROSE FILES

Diane Wald

Regal House Publishing

Published by
Regal House Publishing, LLC
Raleigh, NC 27605
All rights reserved

ISBN -13 (paperback): 9781646035953
ISBN -13 (epub): 9781646035960
Library of Congress Control Number: 2024944622

Cover images and design by © C. B. Royal

Regal House Publishing, LLC
https://regalhousepublishing.com

The following is a work of fiction created by the author. All names, individuals, characters, places, items, brands, events, etc. are either the product of the author's imagination or are used fictitiously. Any resemblance to actual events, places, institutions, persons, current or past, is entirely coincidental.

Printed in the United States of America

For Carey

"Don't call yourself a secret
unless you mean to keep it."

—Leonard Cohen

I Never Changed My Name

My name is Violet Maris and I've done a terrible thing. It didn't start out terrible; it started out clever and intriguing. Only later did I realize how much I'd confused and hurt people, including myself. Only later did I realize there were probably better ways to get things done. At twenty-six, you'd think I would have been smarter about life, but I wasn't. I was the last person anyone would ever suspect of doing such a thing. Almost everyone I knew would have described me as a nice, sane, talented young woman. All that made everything easier, or so I thought.

Just before I embarked upon the venture that eventually doomed me to perpetual regret, I felt I was firmly on the path to becoming woefully unfinished as a human being, one of my greatest fears. I was highly motivated to do something unique, something important, something that would attach to my resumé just the right amount of "reputation." And that was how all the trouble started. Innocently enough, but still.

It's not that I didn't discuss it with anyone; I did that. But only with one person. Unfortunately, either he had the same character flaws that I do, or perhaps he actually believed the idea was sound and worthy of

1

his assistance. I don't know. Maybe he was just excited and didn't give it enough thought. I don't hold it against him, really. I mean, there wasn't anything in it for him, and, if it failed, which of course it did, there wouldn't be any consequences for him either, especially the way things turned out.

I'm not in jail or anything, thank God. I've simply become the exact opposite of what I set out to be. If anyone bothers to think of me at all, I'm thought of as a fool and a poseur. The best I could have hoped for was that I'd be forgotten, that the universe would allow me to take up another line of work and live out my days quietly and humbly in another part of the country, or world. I'm older now. Some good things have happened to me, but purely by accident. I know I'm lucky every time something makes me smile. You'd think I'd be able to relax into anonymity by this time, but that's not the case.

I never changed my name; maybe I should have. It just seemed like too much trouble.

THE WARMTH

At some point when I was a smallish child, I'm not sure exactly when, I started noticing that certain things I touched or picked up seemed warmer than they should have. I'm not talking about picking up a stone that's been baking in the sunlight all day, and I'm only talking about inanimate objects. It didn't matter what they were made of, or whether I had a slight fever or anything scientific like that. Here's an example: one time when I was about seven, I was at my grandma's and she asked me to run upstairs and bring down her hairbrush. I ran upstairs and there it was in all its art-deco glory, nestled among the many fascinating objects on her dressing table. There she displayed her cut-glass camphor bottle, her black and gold Chinese jewelry casket (containing the real coral necklace and earrings she told me I could have when she died), an enameled face powder box with matching pouf, and a tidy pile of embroidered handkerchiefs, pressed and scented with lavender and something else—maybe rose water. I opened the jewelry box and picked up a silvery bracelet, laid it lengthwise along my tiny arm for a few seconds to feel its weight and coolness against my skin, and placed it carefully back in the box. Then I picked up the hairbrush. It was warm, about the temperature of a piece of toast that has just been buttered. I wondered about it, but I was just a kid—lots of things that seemed magical to me then turned out later, upon discussion with adults, to be perfectly normal. And I never thought to mention this warmth to anyone. I just brought the hairbrush downstairs to Grandma. She thanked me, but didn't say a thing about its temperature.

I continued to find warm objects every now and then as I grew up. I never knew what it meant, but I had an eerie feeling that it did mean something, and that some-day I would find out. I only mentioned my secret phe-nomenon to someone once—a lover, actually, as we lay trading secrets in bed one morning—and he couldn't make any sense of it at all. It disturbed him, in fact, and he immediately started wondering what scientific oddity could explain it. All through breakfast he kept handing me small items from the table like the pepper shaker or a jelly spoon or a marigold he'd plucked out of a vase. "Is this hot?" he'd say. "What about this?" Not a single thing was. I tried to explain to him that warm is more subtle than hot, but the whole thing had gotten out of hand, and I begged him to forget about it. About a week later we broke up. I never told him that one day I brought in his mail when I came in his front door and one small beige envelope felt decidedly as if it had been briefly in the oven.

This phenomenon—or aptitude, if you will—has followed me my entire life. I believe now (and this could change, of course, if there's more understanding to be had) that the warmth of an object either foretells or sometimes simply signals happenings in my life that I need to attend to. I'm telling you all this not because it's going to help absolve me of my crimes, but because I don't want to just spring it on you. It's part of who I am, that's all; it's something I recognize.

PHAW, OR, THE HOME

"The Home," as almost everyone called it, instead of PHAW, a somewhat unsavory sounding acronym, was the Provincetown Home for Artists and Writers, a ramshackle but romantic haven for hungry, talented, "emerging" artists and writers that had been founded just a few years before I discovered its existence. I was a budding literary critic for a minor but respected alternative (read "artsy") Boston newspaper at the time, and I had interviewed a young poet named Robert Schneider, who told me he was thinking of applying for a fellowship at The Home, a geographically alluring place that provided an eight-month-long hiatus from real life, where one would be provided a rudimentary dwelling, a modest monthly stipend, and the freedom to pursue—whatever. You could do what you liked; write, paint, sculpt what you liked; consort with the other residents as much or as little as you liked; and not be required to produce any proof of your creativity. Bobby Schneider, by the way, was adorable—in fact, I'm pretty sure he was flirting with me—but I wasn't in the market for such a complication just then. What intrigued me was his reference to The Home, and I began to investigate.

I explored my topic in libraries. Also, I'd met quite a few artistic types through my work, so I made some calls, and those who knew about the place were eager to spill what they knew or had heard. Apparently, even though the facilities weren't pristine and modern, and the stipend didn't quite cover the cost of living, the place already had a noteworthy reputation and fellowship slots were highly coveted. It offered eight months of artistic freedom, starting in October, in a fascinating, unusual town. The selection committee was made up of bonafide creatives, and it wasn't easy to get in. One of the poets, for example, was a Pulitzer Prize winner and one of the painters was a deity in the pantheon of abstract expressionists. It also wasn't snobby; you didn't have to be a "somebody" to get selected. You could be a nobody if they thought you had promise. It was all about the work.

I was more than intrigued. I thought I might have stumbled upon something that could give my embryonic career in journalism a boost. Nobody—yet—was writing about The Home. I also felt that a mere article, or even an artsy/bitchy critique, would not be captivating enough. I realized I'd have to go visit the place, nose around a bit, and see if I could come up with an angle I thought would capture the attention of prospective journalistic venues. I was determined to put in a very deep effort.

Just Passing By

I'd always loved Provincetown. When I was a kid in New Jersey, my parents would rent a cottage in Wellfleet for a week (or sometimes two when they could afford it), and my memories of those vacations are among the sweetest of my childhood. The beaches and the air and the ocean and the food: all of those were delightful, of course, but there was always one day set aside for visiting "Ptown," which I guess my parents considered the epitome of weird, and part of our education. I'm sure they secretly enjoyed it too, and not just the extraordinary saltwater taffy. When I was really little, I didn't even know what made the people who lived there so beguiling. I didn't know any artists or fishermen, and I certainly didn't know what "gay" meant, but I did intuit that there were no restrictions in Ptown on what a person could look like, or be, or even pretend to be. It all looked like tremendous fun. I thought it was a marvel beyond anything New Jersey, or even New York City, could offer. When I was in college I would steal away to Wellfleet or Truro for a weekend now and then with whatever friend or boyfriend would go with me, and then I would take them to Ptown, where most of them had never been before. In addition to the wildly colorful town and its residents, I reveled in the natural atmosphere of the place: fog, sea life, high dunes, pitch pine, ozone. I felt I could breathe more easily. Walking down Commercial Street on a summer night was, for me, a strange kind of heavenly stroll. I didn't belong there, and yet I did.

So it was no hardship at all to pack up my little white Chevy Citation and set out to investigate The Home. I pretty much knew the way by heart. Once I crossed over the Sagamore Bridge, I got that old feeling of freedom and possibilities. It was just about two hours to Provincetown if the traffic was good and you drove really fast.

Somewhere during my drive, I realized to my delight that it was April, and off-season. I hadn't even thought about that. I was able to park easily; quickly secure an inexpensive room in a B&B on charming Bradford Street, complete with a view of the famous Pilgrim Monument; unload my stuff; and set out on foot for The Home. I didn't want to try to get inside the place just yet, even though they had an art gallery that was open to the public. I wanted to just walk by, pretending to mind my own business: just another Ptown off-season visitor on her way to the little supermarket nearby. Buy some pinot noir or a bottle of bourbon. Pick up some of that sweet, spongy Portuguese bread. Maybe a baseball cap that said "Ptown." Just passing by.

I bought the bourbon and bread first, so I'd have

something to carry, and set out down Conwell Street where The Home's three weathered buildings sprawled across an unlined parking lot paved with broken oyster shells. There, a haphazardly parked assortment of vehicles seemed to have stopped mid-sentence while describing where they wanted to go. I walked very slowly. It was about two o'clock in the afternoon and several youngish people stood talking next to one of the vehicles. They were sun-kissed and bohemian. One of them, a long-haired blond man with a sky-blue kerchief tied across his brow, was leaning on an enormous bone that looked like it belonged in the dinosaur exhibit of a natural history museum. A washed-ashore leviathan of the sea, I imagined. The others were talking and laughing in an animated fashion that made me feel lonely somehow. I wanted to be one of them. I walked even more slowly and noted that another building looked like a regular, if downtrodden, house, and the third looked like a barn. Then I had to move on, for fear of being noticed.

I walked back toward town, picked up a coffee and a salty fried fish sandwich at a hole-in-the-wall restaurant, and went back to my room. I ate and drank and lay on the bed staring at the pseudo-historical nautical décor, wondering how I could break into the world of The Home. Knowing the town, I guessed that the best way to meet people was to go to a bar, but I couldn't decide which one. The Figurehead was big and boisterous and on a busy corner, but maybe too popular with any tourists who were taking advantage of the April rental rates. I decided to try Floaters, a seamy, steamy, old-timey bar right on Commercial Street, the main drag, complete with a grimy street-level display window that frightened the tourists away and a bevy of ceiling fans that never seemed to rotate, even in the summer. The name of the place derived from the historical fact that in the 1800s, some fishermen's houses had literally been floated out on barges from Long Point, at the very tip of the Cape, all the way across the bay, because lumber was too scarce and pricey to allow the construction of new homes. I'd been there a couple of times with the friends I'd drag along on my Ptown excursions, and I liked it. The bar itself was usually populated by fish-ermen or other year-rounders in varying degrees of flamboyance and decay. It seemed like the perfect place to find denizens of The Home—or at least discover more about them.

STAR OF THE SEA

"Your name really Violet Maris?" the man said, with a screwed-up expression on his face that would have been appropriate to asking if my name were really Florence Nightingale. I sipped my bourbon.

"Yes," I said.

"You're aware, of course, of the meaning of your last name?"

I looked down the bar at him. There were two unmistakable Ptown locals separating us. One of them had asked me my name, and this character had intercepted the answer. He appeared to be about forty, and was a tad portly, but in that comfortable way some men have that doesn't bother me. He wore prescription-looking sunglasses, a red baseball cap, a dazzlingly white T-shirt, and khaki Bermudas. The shirt was a dead giveaway that he was married; left to their own devices, men never bleach anything. I had to admit he was attractive, with nice features, the kind of guy you could fancy yourself cuddling up to and watching television with. This guy would talk about art and literature all the time, even though he looked like a hockey fan, you could just tell. He was smart, but he probably had some kind of mother fixation or something that could never be addressed. All of this passed through my mind in a matter of seconds. I should have been an FBI profiler I guess. He got up and moved to a stool on the other side of me, so we weren't separated by the other customers.

"Yeah," I said. "I am aware."

He ignored that. "Maris: of Latin origin, meaning 'of the sea,' as in 'Stella Maris,' or 'Star of the Sea,' an epithet for the Virgin Mary. Third declension neuter genitive—indicating possession."

"Yeah. As I indicated, I'm aware."

"Figures that you would be, of course. From now on, if and when I run into you, I will greet you with 'Ave, Stella Maris,' or 'Hail, Star of the Sea.' What a great name to bring to Provincetown." He sighed, clearly pleased with himself.

"Thanks," I said. "Cool." I couldn't tell if this was going anywhere.

"So will I be seeing much of you around here?" he asked.

"I'm not sure," I said. "I'm doing some research."

"Oh boy."

"Is that a problem?"

"No, no," he said, pulling at the brim of his cap. "No problem at all. What are you researching?"

I decided to go for broke. "Well," I said, "are you familiar with The Home?"

He stood up, and stretched. He smiled at me. It was a really nice smile, white teeth on a tanned face. "I am," he said.

"And?"

"I'm on the board there."

"Wow," I said. "Great to meet you. And you are…?"

"Eugene Pelletier. Gene." He pronounced it PELL-uh-teer. "Don't worry. It's French for fur trader, but that's not me at all."

"Okay, then." I looked him over a second time. I just wasn't getting a recognizable vibe, didn't know if I wanted to trust him. "So how long have you been on the board?"

"Right from the beginning. That is to say, not long."

"Were you ever a fellow there?"

He ordered another Jim Beam and one for me. "I was sort of both for a while," he said. "It was all very informal. Now we have committees and all. What's your interest in The Home? And, by the way, is this on the record?"

"No, no," I said. "Sorry. I should have explained. I've just started thinking about writing an article about The Home—freelance. Decided I should come out here and see what people really thought about it—plus, I love the town. Do you think there's any possibility I could interview some staff, or, better yet, some of the fellows?"

Gene Pelletier slowly pulled at his cap again, downed what was left of his bourbon, and stood up next to me. "Miss Maris," he said, "I doubt any of them would want to participate in anything like that. It's kind of a private space for us, you know. Everybody's there to work on their art. Very nice meeting you."

And he was gone. No noise, no drama, just gone as if he had never been there.

The tattooed guy next to me laughed and said, "Sorry, honey. Old Eugene's a little touchy sometimes."

When I got up to leave, I discovered that Gene had slipped his business card under a scarf I'd left folded up on the bar. *Eugene Pelletier*, it said, in a sort of Olde English-y font. *Town Meeting Member, Real Estate Sales, Man about Provincetown*. And there was a phone number. I slipped it into my pocket. It was the temperature of a drinkable cup of tea.

I stayed in town three days. I was able to find four people who lived at The Home, and one who worked there, but every one of them was as closed-mouthed as Gene Pelletier. I didn't call him then, but I thought I might, someday. The whole scenario was frustrating, but it also fueled my desire to find out more. I had to go back to Boston, but I intended to come up with some kind of scheme. I was going to penetrate the sacred wall surrounding The Home, I was sure of it.

THE BEGINNING OF THE END

I discussed this goal over dinner with my dear friend and mentor, Spencer Bayrose. If anyone could help me figure it out, it was Spencer. I'd only known him about ten years, but it seemed like forever. He'd been my college journalism professor and then, a few years later, left academia because of what he called "circum-stantial encumbrances" and miraculously turned up in Boston just as I was looking for a job. He'd landed an editorial position at a big publishing house and was able to convince them to hire me as a junior copy editor. I didn't last very long because I really only wanted to write my own stuff, but my friendship with Spencer was rekindled, and thereafter never waned.

He was eighteen years my senior. He was gay. He was old-school and never mentioned it, so I didn't either. He was tall and elegant, with wavy gray-brown hair, a finely chiseled nose, and lovely, soft blue eyes. His normal speaking voice would put Anthony Hopkins to shame. Sometimes he actually wore an ascot. Even though, as a moderately intelligent and attractive female, I'd had my share of interesting boyfriends, I always felt a little cheated that Spence and I could never be a couple, because we got along so well. Spencer still worked at the publishing house, where he was beloved among his colleagues. He was better read than anyone I'd ever met and could dash off ten exquisite paragraphs at the drop of a hat. He'd hate that I used a cliché like that.

Spence and I had a standing dinner date once a month at a little restaurant in Chinatown called Red Lotus where all the meals featured a kind of fake meat made out of bean curd or something wheaty. It was delicious. There was soft tinkly music on the loud-speakers and the tablecloths were always starched and impossibly white. The dining room was on the second floor overlooking one of the big streets and at night you could drink delicious umbrella-festooned cocktails and watch the Chinese world go by. The night I told Spencer about my hope to write a piece about The Home, I remember we were wolfing down eggrolls at an astonishing rate. He had a napkin tucked in the collar of his shirt. "I know, I know," he said. "I'm sorry this looks so tacky. I just have to protect my favorite tie. It's so old, I'm afraid it will expire before I do if it has to be dry cleaned one more time." The tie was lavender, with a subtle geometric pattern in ivory and mauve. It was exquisite.

He went on, signaling that he'd actually been listening. It was one of the many things I loved about him. "I've heard of The Home, of course," he said, "but I don't know anyone who's been there."

I told him how Gene Pelletier and the others had evaded my questions, and how that made me all the more eager to find out about the place. It was then that Spence came up with the idea that ended up changing my life.

He ordered for both of us: some kind of spicy soup, a vast mound of tri-colored rice with bean-curdy "chicken," and two more drinks with umbrellas. "Violet," he said, "why don't you just apply there yourself?"

I stared at him. He stared back. His eyes said, "Why didn't *you* think of this?" I remembered a phrase from Richard Wilbur: "mad-eyed from stating the obvious." I took the tiny pink umbrella from my drink, stuck it in my hair, and leaned back in my chair.

"No," I said. "Really? But I have no talent. I mean, maybe I'm getting to be a decent journalist, but I'm not a painter or poet or fiction writer. It's a brilliant idea, Spencer, but I'd never get in. That place has high standards."

He laughed. "Well," he said, "maybe there's another way." He couldn't tell me anything more until after dinner, he said, when we'd repair to his apartment for coffee. "Don't let me forget to feed Dusty," he said. "If she doesn't get fed on time she's apt to throw up in my slippers." He was talking about his gorgeous, mostly white, sixteen-year-old Siamese-mix cat, Dusty Springfield. He said he'd named her after the singer because of her mellifluous and insistent voice.

So after dinner we took the T back to his place, a third-floor apartment in a Jamaica Plain triple-decker. It was so lovely: all the original woodwork, oak floors, deep-set windows, a breezy private porch, and, my favorite thing, an oval stained-glass window in the bathroom. There were plants everywhere; he specialized in succulents because the sunlight was so intense on one side of the apartment. The chairs and sofa were faded and squishy, and usually after Spencer fixed us some cappuccino, we'd settle into our customary poses: Spence sprawled out on the sofa amid a flotilla of pillows, and I curled up the in the chair next to him, with a crocheted afghan over my shoulders. Every time I went to his place, I wanted to stay forever.

This time was slightly different, though. Spencer glided into the living room carrying a lacquered tray on which sat two tiny steaming cups, set it down on the table, and said, "Go fetch the biscotti in the kitchen. I'll be right back." I could hear him in his study opening and closing drawers and rifling through papers. Then he came out and ceremoniously presented me with one of those huge accordion files. It was old and brown and falling apart. The cord closure was worn through and the whole thing was held together by what looked like an ancient cowboy string tie.

"What the…?"

"Open it."

The file was quite warm, but I didn't say anything. I untied the tie and peeked inside. Every section was filled to bursting with old typewriter paper, some of it yellowed onionskin. I looked at Spencer.

"Go ahead," he said. "Start anywhere."

I pulled out a couple of pages and turned on the reading lamp over my chair. The print was fading, but as I started to read, I realized I'd fallen into the middle of a remarkable narrative. I was reading about a boy's childhood in the suburbs of Baton Rouge. I read a few paragraphs and stopped. "I have to repeat my original question," I said. "What the…?"

Spencer savored his coffee, and held out the plate of biscotti to me. "Lots of anise," he said, "the way you like them." Then he put his cup down.

"What you have in front of you, my dear, are short stories based on my life. I hate memoirs, so I decided to do it this way. Some of it's true, some's not. I've been pecking away at it forever. It's not finished, of course— but then neither am I." He just kept smiling. Uncharacteristically, he had biscotti crumbs all down the front of his grey and mint green argyle vest. Dusty sauntered into the room, licking her lips after her fresh fish dinner, and leaped gracefully onto the coffee table. She didn't disturb anything there, and Spencer let her stay.

I was stunned. "Are you going to allow me to read this?" I said. "I would love to, of course; I'm just so surprised. I never knew you wrote anything but news articles and feature stories." I actually felt a little dizzy with the oddness of what was happening. Our whole comfortable dynamic had been shifted by a mild underground explosion. I didn't know where to go next.

"I have a timely reason for giving you this, Violet," he said. "Think."

But I was stymied. We sipped and chomped in silence for quite a while, and I finally thought I'd solved the puzzle.

"Oh!" I said. "I get it! You'll apply to The Home and feed me all sorts of information. You'll be my personal spy! I love it, Spence. What an amazing idea!"

He looked crestfallen. "Violet," he sighed. "Please. I'm too old for that sort of thing. YOU will apply, using my writing. Most likely you will get in, because my stories are pretty good, and you will have everything you need right at your fingertips. What do you think?"

This was too much for me. I couldn't get my head around it at first. I'd never done anything even remotely shady or risky before, and this was huge. I was overflowing with questions, and one of them was a little too scary to ask. Spencer obviously thought his writing was good enough to get me accepted into The Home, but was it? I'd have to take his word for it until I could look at it myself, and maybe even, surreptitiously, test it on somebody else, someone with some literary chops.

All I said to Spencer was, "Huh."

He howled with laughter. "Why, Miss Violet," he said, affecting his favorite Tennessee Williams accent. "I have *haahdly evah* found you to be at a loss for words."

After a minute or two I came out of my coma. "But, Spence," I said, "that's so terrifying. I mean, it's brilliant, but I'm not sure I could pull it off, and if I got caught, it would be terrible." Then I had another alarming thought. "And even if I didn't get discovered, and I published an article about my experiences there, everyone I'd met there would hate me—maybe even sue me, I don't know…"

Spencer grabbed Dusty, who was about to step into the middle of the biscotti plate, smooshed her into his lap, and looked at me kindly. "I know," he said. "That's a risk. You'd have to be really, really dedicated to secrecy while you were there and not form any deep personal relationships. You'd have to be sort of standoffish, I think, but that could just be part of your oddball writer's persona. Then when you publish your article, you could disguise people. I'm sure you know how to do that. There would still be some who'd be angry about it, I suppose, but that's show biz."

I sighed. "I don't know, Spence," I said. "Let me think about it. And in the meantime, can I read all this stuff?" I hadn't let go of the big folder the whole time; I realized I was holding onto it very tightly, and little flakes of the cardboard covering were sloughing off on my hands.

"Of course!" he said. He winked. "I'm sure you must be wondering if it's even good enough to get you into a decent prep school. Of course you should read it—as much or as little as you like. Let me know what you think. The rest of it is solely your choice, my dear—choice is the operative word."

We chatted a while more. I overdosed on biscotti. I went home with the big warm brown folder under my arm and my brain sizzling.

Falling into the Files

Naturally I dug into Spence's prose almost immediately. It was mesmerizing. I didn't need anyone else's opinion. Every few paragraphs I had to put it down and stare at the ceiling, wondering why in the world he had kept it under wraps all this time. When he handed it to me, I could tell he knew what it was worth, so it couldn't have been that he was full of self-doubt. The pieces I'd read so far had nothing to do with his sexuality either, but I surmised that all that might come up later, and that perhaps an effort to remain in the closet was at the root of making the piece fiction instead of memoir. But it really didn't matter. They were just so good.

The stories were full of characters with luxurious Southern names like Luther and Arabella and Lance, and their conversations, while ordinary, simmered with meaning and nuance. Nature was everywhere; I hadn't realized how devoted Spencer was to trees and flowers and wildlife. He had moved up north and become a city slicker, but obviously his heart remained with the verdant riverbanks and lace-festooned forests of his youth. His prose made me hungry; in fact, it activated all my senses. After a while I had to set it aside and get some sleep.

I called him first thing the next day. When he picked up, I said, "Spence, this stuff is absolutely wonderful."

There was a long pause. "How much did you read?"

"Enough to feel its brilliance. Why in the world didn't you ever publish any of it?"

He sighed. "I don't know, darling. I just couldn't bring myself to part with it, I guess. I didn't want anyone to see it. But then when I thought of you using it, I was filled with joy. It's my perfect solution—anonymity with a big dollop of friendship involved." He laughed. "Do you know what I mean?"

"I think so," I said, "but I'm going to have to read more of it before I decide. I'm about halfway through the folder. Is there more after that?"

"Tons," he said. "Don't worry about that. There's more than enough to keep you going for quite a while, and anyway, I don't think they monitor your output at that place, do they?"

"True." We signed off.

I kept reading.

BINGEING ANDY GRIFFITH

I read the entire folder, and then experienced a paroxysm of indecision that lasted a couple of months. Spencer never tried to pressure me; he just held my mental hand. The application deadline for The Home was looming. So one day I just tossed all my doubts out the window, filled out the paperwork, and mailed it in.

To apply for a fellowship as a fiction writer, you had to submit a rudimentary application and a twenty-five-page writing sample. You had to promise that, if accepted, you'd live at The Home for the entire eight months of the fellowship, and that everything you said on your application was true. I felt guilty, of course, but I convinced myself that, literally, everything I'd said on the application itself was true—name, address, education, all that. What wasn't true, of course, was that the work I was submitting was my own, but nowhere on the application did it ask you to swear to that. As I said before, this was during The Home's early years. In those days, you didn't even need letters of recommendation. I'm sure their applications are a whole lot stricter now.

I filled out the application, walked down the street, rammed the fat manila envelope into my corner postbox, and then nearly had a heart attack. I actually tried to stick my arm down into the box to retrieve my sins, but of course that didn't work. I jogged home, but when I got to my door, I turned around and jogged down to the nearest bar and had a stiff bourbon. It wasn't even noon. I couldn't even drink it. I went home, called Spencer to confess what I'd done, and went back to bed and watched idiotic television shows all day. I binged an entire season of *The Andy Griffith Show* on some obscure channel I didn't even know existed. Once in a while I would get up and eat cookies. I was terrified.

And of course I was accepted. The gracious letter came about two months later, full of praise for my "fine work," and enclosing all sorts of information about housing and orientation meetings and such. I looked at the left-hand margin of the letter, where all the particulars about The Home were listed. There it was: Eugene Pelletier, Board Chair. Chair, huh. I knew he would remember me, and I knew I'd have to come up with a good cover story before I met him again. In fact, my whole life, for the foreseeable future, would be a cover story, and I'd better become an expert on my new self really fast.

Recipe Prep in Unit 3

Several nervous months loomed before I had to move to The Home, and I went into serious training. I wanted to feel different, so I got a drastic haircut. As I watched my long dark-blond curls fall to the stylist's floor, I felt as if I were preparing to go into a convent. I ended up still looking pretty good, though, even for a postulant. My face had, as my mother always told me, "good bones."

My partner in crime and I met every few days to refine our scheme. With Spence as my coach, I tried to become him—as a writer. He filled me in on the background for each story, since they were, as he'd originally told me, quite autobiographical. I wasn't planning on sharing this information unless I had to, but we both thought there might be times when deep conversations with the other writing fellows would necessitate some amount of sharing. One thing I would certainly be asked about was why I wrote all the stories from the point of view of someone of the opposite sex. That wasn't too hard; I could fake it. I just wanted to be prepared.

I desperately wanted to contact some journals that specialized in the kind of interpretive article I was interested in writing before I embarked on the project, but it was too risky. Writers of all types are notoriously garrulous, I knew, and all it would take to ruin my secret mission was for the word to get out while I was still at The Home. I poked around a lot though. It seemed to me that such an exposé would be welcomed by several publications, a couple of them quite prestigious. I would have to keep my eyes on that prize, even when things became difficult, as I was sure they would.

Eventually, the day came when I had to pack up my car with eight months' worth of deceit and set out for the Cape. I sublet my apartment for the duration. It was time to go.

I arrived at The Home during a crushing downpour. I dripped all over Betty the office manager's desk, but she was sweet and welcoming and gave me the key to unit 3, the funky efficiency apartment that would be my temporary digs, and which would host so many important moments in my new secret life. She reminded me about the orientation luncheon the next day and then suggested that I not unload my car in the current deluge, but go have lunch in town and come back in a while when the rain might have let up a bit. "October is schizoid here, weatherwise," she said. "You'll get used to it."

So I did that, even though I was a mass of raw nerves already. I hadn't even met anyone but Betty and I was already feeling sweaty and paranoid. I found a fairly deserted little restaurant at the far end of Commercial Street (I wasn't ready to run into Gene again) and ordered an omelet, but couldn't eat much. I had a beer, which I thought would settle my stomach, but I don't like beer, and it didn't. Gradually, though, the rain did begin to taper off, so I drove back to my fate. By that time, a couple of other new residents were checking in. It didn't take me long to unload the Chevy, even though unit 3 was on the upper tier of apartments. We newbies smiled and waved at each other in the parking lot, but I guess everyone was waiting until the orientation luncheon the next day to really get acquainted. Fine by me. I wanted some aspirin.

Unit 3 was small and rustic, with a tiny kitchen and tinier bathroom. It was spotlessly clean, though. I unboxed my sheets and towels, made up the bed, and then unpacked the tiny black-and-white television I'd vacillated about bringing, praising the gods for convincing me to do so. The reception was terrible (and, I learned later, would never get much better, even in good weather), but it provided another voice in the room, a voice that couldn't challenge me or say anything too personal. I had also packed a bottle of red wine and a couple of sandwiches, so I didn't have to go out for dinner. I was in hiding. I knew tomorrow would end all that. I sprawled out on the lumpy futon and watched static-crackling TV until about nine o'clock, ate my paltry dinner, and began placing a few preliminary notes for my article in a folder labeled "recipes," which I hid in my sock drawer. Then I got into bed and fell fast asleep instantly.

I wondered if all this secrecy would render me old and exhausted before my time.

CORDELIA, PHRANK, AND GENE

First thing the next morning, I called Spence from a phone booth on Commercial Street and left a message saying, "I'm here and I'm scared, but all is well. Orientation luncheon today. Call you later." I made some coffee and put the rest of my stuff away, although that only took about ten minutes. The joys of simplicity. I showered, got dressed, and bravely opened the door to the little boardwalk that led to the stairs. It was a gorgeous autumnal Cape Cod day: brilliant and windy and smelling of brine and pine and fallen leaves. As I passed the nearby door of unit 2, a woman stepped out and said, softly, "Hey. Hi."

I turned and looked at her. She was very thin and rather delicate looking, probably a bit older than me. Her hair, ear-length and very curly, was colorless—I mean to say it might have been light brown or it might have been grey or it might have been transparent. In the extreme sunlight, you just couldn't tell. She was smiling, and I smiled back. She proffered a thin white hand. "Cordelia Hight," she said. Her hand fluttered into and out of mine briefly, like a confused moth.

"Violet Maris."

"Oh, *VI*-o-let! I adore that name!" Cordelia slipped

past me and floated down the stairs. She was wearing a wispy flowered kimono over a sweatshirt and jeans. I had no idea what to think.

I followed Cordelia into the common room, where the welcome luncheon was to take place. Clearly she had already met several of the new fellows, since she launched effortlessly into a kind of hesitant conversation with two women and a man who were standing near the back of the room, sipping what appeared to be orange juice out of clear plastic cups. When I say "hesitant," I mean that Cordelia's conversational style, with which I was to become intimately acquainted, was a series of syllables and sighs and little feminine laugh noises, all punctuated by excessive rolling of her large and slightly protuberant eyes. The total effect was rather pretty, but in an unnerving way. Months later, one of her many romantic partners would tell me, cruelly, "You wanted to feed her, or comb her hair, or slap her, or comfort her, or give her vitamins, but ultimately you just fucked her, because that's all she ever seemed to want."

I took a seat at the second table and soon a giant of a man with a well-groomed black beard joined me. He wore an old army jacket with several military badges on it and a white shirt with a striped tie. It must have been some kind of statement, but I'm not sure of what. He was another fiction writer, I soon found out, named Phrank. "With a PH." Ah.

Then the room began filling up and we all took seats. I found myself between Phrank and Cordelia. The writing coordinator, a small blond preppy-looking woman who mystified us by apologizing for having "no credentials to speak of" appeared at a makeshift podium, cranked up an antiquated overhead projector, and began talking through a series of really boring transparencies. Not what I'd expected at all. I'm not sure exactly what I did expect. Really not that though.

Phrank leaned over and whispered, "Wanna get a drink after lunch?"

I nodded.

Lunch was cold cuts on French bread, salad, and seltzer or orange juice. We all mingled for a while afterward and I discovered the orange juice could be enhanced by simply introducing oneself to a Mr. Bill Ebbelow—or Bilbo, as he liked to be called. Bilbo was a painter and head of the visual arts program, but attended every event at The Home because he thought they were all "too fussy" and it was his self-appointed assignment to liven things up. He had a bottle of vodka in his fringed leather shoulder bag, and he'd pour a little into any glass anyone showed him. After a while he just left the bottle open on a side table and pretty soon it was empty. I spied Phrank across the room and raised one eyebrow quizzically, one of my minor talents. He winked and gestured toward the door.

Pretty soon we were out of the parking lot and on

our way into town. We ended up at the Figurehead and I didn't complain. All I wanted was some simple conversation. I didn't get it. It seemed that Phrank's idea of having a drink with someone was extremely literal: you go somewhere with someone and you both drink a drink. He was so hard to talk to that I quickly gave up, downed my bourbon, patted him on the back, and said, "See ya' back at The Home sometime."

"Hey, yeah," said Phrank. At least he smiled.

I was strolling back down Commercial Street when I saw a familiar baseball hat coming my way. Gene Pelletier. He was glowing with friendliness.

"Hail, Stella Maris!" he exclaimed, drawing me into a huge, clumsy hug. "I just can't believe this. I had no idea you were going to apply to The Home. You said you wanted to write an article about it!"

"You've got a good memory," I said, disentangling myself from his embrace. A piece of my hair had fastened awkwardly to a strip of Velcro on his jacket. "Yeah, I lied about that," I continued. "I mean, you just can't trust a writer; you must have realized that by now." I smiled warmly; I was surprised that I really felt friendly toward him now that he was here in front of me. I'd been afraid to meet him again, but that fear now seemed absurd.

He took a step back and looked at me. "You look good," he said. "You look happy. I think you'll like it here."

"Thanks, Gene," I said. "I think so too. This is just day one, though. Check back with me in a month or so," I joked.

"I will," he said, "but I'm sure we'll be running into each other a lot before a month goes by. This town, especially off-season, is like an ongoing family reunion. You really can't avoid anybody, so you might as well not try. That's my experience, anyway." He looked a little goofy. I still thought he was cute though.

"I get it," I said. "Keep your secrets to yourself, huh?" I had no idea why I said it.

He laughed, then continued on down the street. "Right," he said. "You got it."

I liked that Gene wasn't one of those people you couldn't get rid of. He knew when to make his exit.

Verbals and Visuals

Several weeks later, I sat drinking a cup of strong coffee at the rough-hewn, paint-spattered table that served as my desk, a few broad planks balanced on two sawhorses. My chair had probably done its first tour of duty in a kitchen about forty years ago. It was sturdy, with most of the varnish worn off, but the thick life-saver boat cushion I'd found at an amazing store in town called Maritime Miscellany made it comfortable enough. The makeshift desk supported my clunky old Selectric pretty well, and there was plenty of room for assorted papers and cups of coffee and glasses of beer or something stronger. Nothing to complain about, really.

It was a Tuesday morning, very early. I was a lifelong early riser, but no one else would be up for ages, I knew. I looked out the somewhat grimy window over my workstation and wished this apartment had a bay view, but the sky over the cemetery was compensation enough. "Red in the morning, sailor's warning," wasn't that it? I was the sailor, taking good notice. Red and lavender clouds skidded around in the sky and then moved swiftly across the horizon in the almost ever-present cooling breeze of this coastal town. Even if it rained a bit, I might walk down to the harbor later in the day, or maybe even out to the dunes, where the tick population and its vexing agility terrified me. They were everywhere, they were tinier than tiny, and you never knew if there was still one left hiding out in some forsaken crevice on your body. I could tuck my growing-back hair up in a cap and wear long pants, but I didn't want to. I much preferred bare legs and the wind all about my face.

Around eleven I'd usually walk down to the post office, and hope to find a letter—or, better yet, a large manila envelope—from Spencer. His communications had seemed a bit different of late—less enthusiastic and less intimate somehow—but I figured both of us were just easing into a sort of rhythm with this new and furtive back-and-forth. I wished the mail could be sorted earlier because in the late morning I would frequently run in to someone I knew who would ask me why I rented a post office box when I could get my mail at The Home like everybody else. What was so special and secret that I needed this extra layer of privacy? I'd made up a couple of stories, but no one seemed satisfied. It was that kind of place. People were nosey. Or maybe just bored. I couldn't blame them. It's not me, I would say, it's my mother. I handle her financial affairs and she's paranoid about mail getting stolen. Or it's just a quirk, I'd say, it gives me a reason to walk into town and I love the surprise of opening the little old-timey filigreed mailbox door with its tiny key.

I always expect something marvelous will pop out, I'd say, and try to laugh charmingly. Who knows if anyone bought it. Anyway, I had to have that private box.

That little mail cubbyhole held the means to my nefarious end. I would smuggle Spence's envelopes home and retype the stories. Should any of my colleagues visit me during my writing hours, they'd find me pecking away. I was careful not to let anything look suspicious, and I even shredded Spence's manuscripts into tiny pieces and wrapped them in wet newspaper before throwing them in the trash. I'd heard that, toward the end of one's fellowship, we'd be encouraged to submit our writing to the annual "yearbook" publication of The Home. I hoped that was far off into the future, since the idea of attaching my name in print to Spence's work terrified me.

Oh yes, "writing hours." We all posted them diligently on our doors, but after the first couple of weeks no one really bothered about them too specifically, and the signs got scribbled over or taped over or taken down altogether. Sometimes there would even be little hand-drawn cartoons or captioned photos or other amusing things. A flower, maybe, or a tuft of beach grass. It was often sweet. But we pretty much avoided one another all morning and halfway into the afternoon, and after that all bets were off. Of course, there were days when we'd plan excursions, like driving, all of us stuffed into two or three cars, to Hyannis for a movie or some other injection of more-or-less normal civilization, but most days were spent in our apartments or studios until the sun was well on its way down.

After sunset, there were informal parties, or, rarely, more formal PHAW-sanctioned events that usually accompanied art show openings or the like. Sometimes small groups of fellows would wander down to the beach to sit and talk on the damp greyish sand before sashaying absentmindedly into the various bars. Nobody had much money, but we all knew how to make a drink last, and since The Home ran mostly off-season, the friendly proprietors seemed happy enough to let us linger. Sometimes they even joined us and regaled us with stories of the town.

Local residents frequented the bars too, several of whom were attracted to us artistic types. They were mostly men, and mostly alcoholic, but a couple of them, like Harold O'Brien, were pretty interesting. Harold had been (according to him) apprenticed to a famous painter who lived in town for years before committing suicide. Harold (don't dare call him Harry) had ten or twelve of this painter's canvases in his cruddy old apartment and would escort anyone there to view them on short notice. I went with him once, accompanied by another fellow, and was astonished by the quality of the paintings. Harold would not reveal the painter's name, and some people surmised they were his. No one knew the truth, or probably ever would.

By this time, of course, I'd met all the other fellows, both writers and fine artists. We called ourselves "verbals" and "visuals"—it was just more fun. Some of the visuals were hard to get to know, but the verbals were, of course, overflowing with words almost all the time, so making friends was easy. I was especially drawn to a woman poet named Jeanette Lively, who hailed from Hawaii of all places, but who had grown up near New York. She was tiny, that's the only word for her. I doubt she actually attained the five feet that she claimed, but she was fascinatingly petite in every way. Small features, small bones, very short auburn hair—kind of an elfin look altogether. Men swarmed around her. I found her fragility intimidating at first (I'm an average-to-large person, depending on your point of view), but then I found out how down-to-earth and just plain nice she could be. Had I met Jeanette under any normal circumstances, I would have been thrilled with this new friendship, but at The Home I knew I could never relax completely or reveal too much about myself. I had to be faithful to loneliness at all times. I figured that eventually Jeanette would become frustrated with such withholding, but at least for now we were having a lot of fun.

Jeanette lived on the ground floor in unit 10 with her mother. Yep, mother. A very weird thing. Unit 10 was a larger apartment that was reserved for the occasional artist or writer couple that The Home accepted, but

Jeanette had submitted a special petition to bring her mother with her. When I first heard of this anomaly, I figured that Jeanette's mother must have been lame or deaf or in need of Jeanette's constant care for some physical malady, but that wasn't the case. Christine Lively was whole and sane. She was just poor. She and Jeanette had never lived apart, and when Jeanette accepted her fellowship, she, the sole support of the two of them, had had to give up their apartment. Again, these were the early days of The Home; I doubt any arrangement like that would be sanctioned now.

Anyway, Christine was content to keep to herself most of the time, so it took me quite a while to get to know her even a little. Jeanette didn't say much about her mom, and never anything negative. Christine took care of the apartment and the cooking and even adopted a little terrier she named J.D. Salinger to keep her company while her daughter and her fellow fellows were doing whatever fellows do. Christine and J.D. took long walks every day, often coming back with armfuls of beach flora that had dried out in the sun. Christine made charming arrangements of these fuzzy stalks and stems and eventually The Home would ask her to supply some to decorate art openings and board meetings.

Besides Jeanette, there were five other verbals and a passel of visuals. Verbals included the aforementioned Cordelia Hight (poet), Phrank Liddy (fiction); Valda, a

Latvian science fiction writer; and two poets, Anna and Tony, who seemed to have fallen deeply in love with one another during the first five minutes of their residency. They were fairly inseparable and hard to get to know. They spun around attached to one another like twin tops. Among the visuals were painters Allan and Allen (dubbed A1 and A2), a sexy marble sculptor named Bill, a fiber artist named Cora, and a woman named Eeen who made quilts out of everything in sight. They were extraordinary, but I was afraid of Eeen. She was a little creepy and I could imagine her sneaking into our rooms at night and stealing bits of our hair, clothing, and souls to weave into her quilts. And it wasn't just the name, for which she offered no explanation, even when asked directly, or her general aura of spookiness, but the fact that she was a starer. Once she locked onto your face with her kohl-rimmed eyes, you were a goner. There was nothing you could do but leave the room.

STINKING SQUID

I was getting more than a little concerned about Spencer. The notes he enclosed with his pieces just seemed off. Very, very brief. They weren't on Post-it notes, but they could have been. So, one day I just called him. I walked all the way down to the other end of town and found a lunch place with a pay phone on the wall near the restroom. He didn't answer.

That was odd, because I'd picked a day and time when I was pretty sure he'd be home, but I left a message on his machine. "Spencer! It's me. I miss you and I'm getting a weird feeling about things. I'm going to call you around eight tonight, okay? Hope to talk to you soon." I never wanted Spence to call me at The Home, because people would then know that he existed. Everything seemed too risky.

I walked all the way back to the same place at eight and ordered the "special soup of the day" so I could stay a while at the table. The bowl of soup was full of raw clams, which I hated, but the homemade bread that went with it was delicious. I dropped two slices into my jacket pocket for later.

Then I called Spence again. He answered on the first ring, and I knew immediately that there was trouble.

"Lovey," he said, "I'm so tired. It's great to hear your voice, but I'm so tired."

The phone receiver in my hand suddenly became almost too warm to hold. I was sweating. A hippie-ish woman with long pheasant feather earrings approached, clearly eager to use the phone, and I waved her off. I held my hand over the mouthpiece and whispered to her, "Emergency." Sweetly, she backed off. It really was a compassionate town, at least off-season.

"What's wrong, Spence? I knew there was something…"

"I don't know for sure," he said, breathing raggedly, "but I think I'm sick."

"Flu?"

"No, worse."

"Please, Spence. Tell me."

"Sweetie," he said, "do you think we could talk about something else for a while? I'll hear back from the doctor tomorrow. Until then I want to pretend I'm just tired."

"Of course."

For two or three minutes we talked about—I have no idea what. I had sweated through my shirt and could feel rivulets of perspiration running down my back. I said goodbye to Spence, threw some money on the table, and walked back toward The Home the long way, along the shoreline. I took off my shoes and waded into the edge of the icy water. A god-awful stench wafted off a rotting pile of cut-up squid some fisherman had left behind. Gulls screeched with chilling exuberance as they ripped into the carnage. I began to cry.

SANDWORMS

Fishermen. They were everywhere. Obviously, professional fisher-folk were the lifeblood of the year-round town, but tourists and the somewhat less touristy full-summer residents made up a huge portion of the angling that went on every day, both off the harbor boats and along the shoreline. On almost every oceanside beach, surfcasters whipped long nylon lines beyond the whitecaps from thirteen-foot rods with a satisfying whirr and snap, their pants legs rolled up and their sunburned faces fairly quivering with this singular whiff of wildness.

Phrank wanted to take me fishing. You have to understand: even though we all had writing fellowships and all the time in the world to write, no one (or no one I've ever met, at any rate) can write *all* the time. When you don't have to work at a job with regular hours, there are lots of irregular hours to fill.

Phrank had turned out to be a lot of fun. After our initial awkward drink at the Figurehead, I got to know him a bit better. He had a wicked sense of humor and was fairly sexy in an offbeat way. He was really tall, and I liked tall. He had nice skin and freckles. He was smart, and I liked smart. In our infrequent fiction workshops he was astute, kind, and detached enough in his critiques that you could tell he had no agenda or academic arrogance. At The Home, our writers' workshops were segregated into poetry and fiction for no reason I could fathom. I would have been very interested to hear what the poets were doing, but it wasn't to be.

Sometimes guest writers ran the workshops. Fellows were encouraged to suggest writers we loved to visit and work with us, but most of them were too famous and too busy to come. Some of the writing fellows betrayed their ignorance by requesting that The Home invite deceased writers. I found this hilarious; so did Phrank. But we kept our cool. It was another thing I liked about him. Jeanette said he was "a gentleman and a hoot," and I had to agree.

One of the guest writers who did visit was someone I'd requested, so I was charged with showing him around the town, taking him grocery shopping (he was staying in The Home's guest apartment for a week), and serving as general guide and factotum. He was a novelist already well into his eighties and a bit shy. Unfortunately, we just didn't get along that well, but I'm sure it had something to do with the fact that I was a complete fraud and couldn't relax around him. Our best time together was during a shopping expedition at the Acme Supermarket, where we stood together for a long time in the produce aisle discussing the various methods of cooking artichokes. I still use his preferred method of steaming them.

So, anyway, Phrank wanted to go fishing. He figured he could borrow a couple of surf rods for us from Craig, one of the men on the maintenance team for The Home. I said I would rather just go along for the fresh air and scenery, and that I'd provide a nice picnic lunch for us, but Phrank wasn't having any. Unfortunately, I'd already told him how my father had taught me and my brother to fish when we were kids—surf-casting included—so he said I had to at least advise him about all the stuff I'd learned from my dad, and that if I caught anything, he'd reel it in for me, gently remove the hook, and throw it back. Unless it was a bluefish, he said; those he would bring back for dinner. I said okay reluctantly, having lost my childhood enthusiasm for fishing, and advised him that the first thing he'd have to do was get some fresh bait. Probably sandworms, I said, those millipede-ish squirmies that saltwater fish seemed to adore. Ugh.

We drove down to Orleans on a nice cloudy fishing day, planning to set ourselves up on Nauset Beach. I remembered that my dad used to buy fresh sandworms from a little place behind one of the big hotel restaurants on Route 6, so we parked along a side road and I pointed out the bait store to Phrank. It was about a city block away, but you could see it easily from where we had parked. He strode off enthusiastically with his little bait bucket. I saw him approach a doorway and then I realized he had passed by the bait shop and was talking to someone at the back door of the hotel. He was back in five minutes, bucket empty. "Very funny," he said.

"No, no, Phrank, you have to believe me," I spluttered. "I sent you to the right place; you just overshot the bait shop door."

By this time, he was laughing too, imitating the hotel employee who'd dealt with him. "Sandworms, sir? Do you mean for lunch? I'm not sure; I'll check with the kitchen." Phrank swore the poor kid was trying very hard to be polite.

We drove over to Rock Harbor and found some less exotic bait at a sporting goods store there, then back to Nauset. By this time the clouds had tripled and it was freezing cold on the windy beach. Phrank gave me his lined denim jacket to wear over my two sweaters, but I was still cold, and he, of course, was blue. We fished for about an hour, catching nothing (as I'd hoped), and then packed up and headed for midtown Orleans. We settled in at a dark booth in an unpopular-looking bar and grinned at each other, using the red-and-white-checked napkins to wipe the salt spray from our faces.

No Hanky-Panky

Once we warmed up, Phrank and I felt better. We had a couple of beers, split an order of fried clams and onion rings, and gradually peeled off most of our wintery layers until we once again resembled our former artist-colony selves.

Phrank got brave. "I really like you, Violet," he said.

"I like you too," I said. "It's nice to have a fishing buddy."

He laughed, and looked down at his hands, which were folded around his beer glass as if it were a chalice of consecrated wine.

"You know what I mean," he said.

"I think so. And I'm flattered. But I have to tell you that when I got accepted to The Home I promised myself there would be no hanky-panky whatsoever. I just want to work on my stories. I haven't had a relationship, or even a decent dalliance, in a long time, and I intend to keep things that way. That's why, in case you're wondering, I keep to myself a lot—except with Jeanette and her mom, you know?"

He nodded, grinning ruefully. "Yeah," he said. "Too bad."

I thought it was probably time to leave, so we paid

up and bundled ourselves back into Phrank's ancient Pontiac for the trip back to Ptown. It wasn't a bad trip—not even that awkward—but I knew in my heart that something important had shifted. He played the radio really loud, so we didn't have to talk that much. When we got to the PHAW parking lot and Phrank handed me my picnic basket from the back seat, I noticed that the handle was as warm as a kitten's belly.

POTATOES

I waited an extra day before calling Spence again. I knew he was expecting bad news, and I told myself I wanted to give him some privacy, but really I was just scared. Bad news probably meant cancer, I thought, but that wasn't necessarily a death sentence. I mean, with treatment, he might have some good years left. Or maybe it was his heart, I tortured myself. Yeah, it was probably cancer or heart, because otherwise he wouldn't have sounded so...tired. Well, there were treatments for heart disease too. I never even considered another obvious reason Spence might be ill.

The phone rang a long time and then Spence picked up. He didn't sound that bad. He told me right off that he had just finished a huge breakfast, including some "marvelous" home fries. We talked about potatoes for a minute or two—how we both loved them almost any way they were prepared—and then Spence simply said, "Violet." The way he said it killed me. It was possibly the most intimate, the most terrifying way my name had ever been spoken.

"What's happening, Spencer? Just tell me, okay?"

"It's not a simple diagnosis," he said.

"Tell me piece by piece if it's easier. What made you go to the doctor in the first place?"

"I've just been feeling generally awful," he said. "Sweaty and chilly all at the same time. Bleeding gums sometimes, though I take good care of my teeth. My eyes are weird and I can't fit my contacts in properly. Heart palpitations. No appetite."

"And?"

"They did a lot of the usual blood tests, which were inconclusive, and then they tested me for HIV."

I dropped the receiver, which had become boiling hot. I picked it up off the floor. "Wow," I said. "I've read about that a bit."

You have to understand that in those days—the early eighties—AIDS and HIV were in the news, but I'm ashamed to say I wasn't all that well informed about the subject—or any other news for that matter. I rarely even bought a newspaper. Back in Boston, I'd heard that some gay men were really worried about it, and here in Ptown it was a fairly common topic. Lots of men, it seemed, were becoming infected and there was a general unease. I didn't personally know anyone who'd been diagnosed, but I didn't really hang out with anyone who wasn't at The Home. I remember hearing that some movie star died of it, and other famous people, like Elizabeth Taylor, were raising money for research. Everyone was upset with the government for basically ignoring the problem. But I was pretty much deeply stupid on the subject, selfishly immersed in my own drama. Soon I would learn the depth of my stupidity.

Spence sighed. "Well, darling," he said, "not only am I positive for HIV, but the doctor also said my symptoms are worrisome. And there are some, Violet, that I'm too shy to tell you about, and some labels that I just don't want to use. The outlook is, shall we say, grim." He had switched to his professorial voice to compensate for all the emotion. I could hear him swallowing with difficulty.

"But there must be treatments, right? Things they can try that will help you?" By this time, I was sitting on the floor. There were chairs at a table nearby that I could have pulled over, but it didn't occur to me. The floor was clean at least, because I felt as if I were sinking into it.

"Violet," he said, "not really. I got the impression they can make me feel more comfortable for a while, but there's no cure of course, and…"

"It's going to be all right," I said. Because I was without a doubt the most obtuse, meanest person in the world.

"No, sweetie, it's not."

"No?" I steeled myself.

"No." There was a pause. "But we'll carve out some time together, okay? You can come visit me whenever you want, and at some point maybe I can come down there and visit you. I'd love to see Provincetown again, and I'd love to roll up my trousers and stick these miserable old feet in some salt water and eat fresh clams."

We left it that way. I would go see him soon. And nothing would ever be the same again.

WORKING ON MY RECIPES

I hadn't expected Spence to keep sending me his stories, but he did. The envelopes arrived regularly. Spence seemed, in fact, to be feeling a bit better since his diagnosis, and he'd gotten treatment for some of the symptoms he was suffering—no cure, as he constantly reminded me, but at least some temporary relief. I was planning to drive up to see him in Boston in a week or so. Then, if all went well, he'd visit me on the Cape as the weather started to get warm, just before my fellowship came to an end.

We were about halfway through the fellowship term now, and although I felt things were going more or less smoothly, I definitely had a sense that time was speeding up. I could tell that the other fellows too were realizing that this glorious free time really would end, and that they'd better get serious and get down to work. There was a bit less socializing; there was a bit more regard for each other in terms of our art. The visuals were working furiously in their studios; you could smell paint and clay and solder quite distinctly. When you walked past the door of a verbal's apartment, you could hear feverish typing, or sometimes just silence backed up by classical music.

As for me, though, the only thing that was escalating (except for my excruciating anxiety about Spencer's health) was that I was working harder on making notes in my "recipes" folder for possible inclusion in the article I would someday write about The Home. I had begun to realize that Spence and I had given no attention to exactly what I would do when I left Ptown and how I would begin to peddle my exposé. But I knew I could no longer depend on Spence for this sort of advice; he was engaged in a far more critical battle.

In our fiction workshops, "my" pieces garnered high praise. Phrank and Valda were especially intrigued. My relationship with Phrank was still friendly, but of course things were just a tiny bit strained since our fishing expedition. Valda loved the pieces I submitted because, I think, their Southern-flavored exoticism somehow soothed her homesickness for Latvia. Oddly, my friend Jeanette was only minimally interested in my work, since poetry was her One True Love. Her mother Christine was another story. Jeanette would pass my work along to her mom, and Christine would compliment me and try to engage me in conversations about the stories whenever she could. She would also gaze at me strangely. Or so I thought. I asked Jeanette about that and she said no, her mother was just the intense type, and didn't have much else to interest her in Ptown. So I tried to be gracious and make up stuff about the stories to entertain Christine. I told her I'd done a lot of research into Louisiana, that I'd even taken a trip down there. I lied. I didn't like doing it, but I lied and lied.

JEANETTE AND PHRANK

Jeanette and Phrank became a couple. I guess I just wasn't paying enough attention to everything going on around me, so I was surprised one night when a few of us gathered in a booth at Floaters, and I noticed Phrank casually stroking Jeanette's back and pushing her hair away from her forehead in an intimate way when she was talking. "Can't see your eyes." He smiled at her. She smiled back. Nobody else seemed to think anything of it.

Phrank left early, so I walked back to The Home with Jeanette. "Sooooo," I said, trying to sound casual. "Something going on with you and Phrank?"

She stopped walking, sat down on the curb, and lit a cigarette, a rarity for her. "Jesus Christ, Violet, I thought you'd never notice!" We both started laughing.

"I'm so sorry. I guess I've been pretty distracted these days. When did all this start?"

She grinned. "Well, not long after the two of you went fishing." We started giggling again.

"Oh nooooo,' I said.

"I would have told you right away, but there was this tiny voice in the back of my head whispering that your feelings might be hurt...or something. I know that's stupid. I don't know; maybe I just felt shy. It started up kind of all of a sudden. My car stalled in the parking lot and Phrank came out with a magic screwdriver and got it started. I was really grateful. I was just going out to Race Point to take a walk, so I asked him to come along. We had a great time and when we got back, Mom invited him to stay for dinner. The rest is history."

"Wow," I said. "That's great. So you really like him?" I started to feel jealous—not of them, but of lovers in general. It had been a while. And I'd sworn off fraternizing with the other residents, or even anyone in town.

"I do," she said. "I'm not sure if it will last, but it's really sweet now. I feel a little guilty leaving Mom alone so much, but I need this."

"She'll be fine," I said. "She'll understand. And, if it'll help, I'll try to spend a little time with her in the evenings."

What the hell was I saying? Jeanette perked right up.

"Oh, if you could, Violet, that would be wonderful! She likes you so much, and she likes to talk to you about your work."

I smiled. Jeanette smiled. Oh boy.

More Red Lotus

I drove up to Boston to see Spence one afternoon, planning to drive right back that evening, but he was so eager to talk and eat and laugh that I decided to spend the night on his cozy sofa and drive back at dawn. With Dusty sprawled out on top of me, I had a lot of time to think. I didn't sleep much. Spence was a bit thinner, and didn't look bad overall, but I could tell how tired he was. He was still working, and no one at his job knew anything about his health. Even to me, he didn't seem to want to talk about it much. I had, of course, a million questions, but I knew that most of them would embarrass Spence, so I held back. For now, I told myself, the best thing I could do for him was be his friend and take my cues from him.

That night Spence didn't feel up to going all the way into Chinatown for a meal, so I enlisted the help of a friend who lived downtown, telling her only that Spence had a terrible case of the flu and I couldn't leave him. She graciously delivered a huge bag of takeout goodies from our favorite restaurant. Unfortunately, Spence wasn't too hungry, and I ended up eating a great deal of it myself. Spence went to bed early, and I repaired to the sofa. All night I could hear his labored breathing and restless turning over and over in the other room. I left early in the morning, taking with me, at Spence's insistence, an assortment of leftovers in a big, garish Red Lotus shopping bag. He gave me the most amazing hug I'd ever had from him—none of that peck-peck on each cheek nonsense.

When I got back to The Home it was almost dinner time. I ran into Gene Pelletier in the parking lot as I unpacked; he was just exiting a board meeting. "Hail, Stella Maris," he said, predictably. He never tired of it.

"Gene," I said. "Nice to see you."

He paused before getting into his Land Rover. What a cool vehicle, I thought. It was an old classic model, sort of a greyish-blue, with a big spare tire right on the hood. It had flappy canvas things on the sides with oddly shaped, zippered windows that looked like isinglass, but I guess were some kind of plastic. My father had always wanted a car like that, but there wouldn't be much use for it as a family vehicle. "Looks like you've been away," he said, eyeing my overnight bag and the food-laden shopping bag with Chinese symbols on it.

"Yeah. Visited a friend in Boston." I had a sudden and incomprehensible impulse. "Do you like Chinese food?" I guess I thought I'd just hand him the bag.

"*DO* I?" he said. "But, I have to ask, is that bag by any chance from Red Lotus?"

"It is!" I said. "You know it?"

"Oh my god, Violet. What's in the bag? No, never

mind. I'll give you a thousand dollars for it!" He pulled off his baseball hat and made a deep, gentlemanly bow. He was pretty adorable.

"Wow," I said. "What are the chances that a bigshot board chairman like yourself would be humbled by his addiction to bean curd?"

"I'm serious about the thousand bucks," he said.

"Give me fifteen minutes to get myself together and then come up to unit 3 and I'll share it with you."

Gene put his hat back on and folded his hands in front of him as if praying. "See you in fifteen," he said, and jumped into his vehicle. As I was dragging my stuff up to my apartment, I could hear a Neil Young song blasting from his radio. Maybe he wasn't old in spirit.

I Become the Bee's Knees

Honestly, I'm not sure how it all happened. When Gene appeared at my door, precisely fifteen minutes later, he was hoisting an expensive-looking bottle of saké in a sort of salute. I wondered how he'd obtained it so fast. "Thank you," he said, "for saving me from a night of lonely reheated chicken."

He further explained that his wife, Hannah, had gone off to visit her relatives on the mainland, and had left him a dish of what he called "boiled fowl" in the fridge. The mention of the word *wife* gave me momentary pause, but I dismissed it. All we were doing was sharing a meal. This happened all the time, with all sorts of combinations of people. Food, conversation, fun, that's all.

Gene and I sat down at my tiny all-purpose table and fell on the reheated Red Lotus food as if we hadn't eaten in days. Actually, there wasn't as much of it as I'd thought, so I guess the carefully warmed saké had an even more intense effect on us than it might have had otherwise. I could tell Gene didn't want to leave, and I didn't want him to. I turned on my little TV and, miracle of miracles, locked onto a station showing some kind of forties' movie. I think Jimmy Stewart was in it, but I can't really say. I joined Gene as he slipped smoothly over to my lumpy sofa-futon and took off his thermal fishing vest to reveal a peach-colored long-sleeved T-shirt. Just before he pulled me over to him and kissed me, I remember thinking what a surprising color that was for him to wear. I liked it.

And I liked everything we did that night. My first impressions of Gene were true: he was sweet and cozy and smart as a lover. He didn't talk much, but he was kind. I did wonder if this was something he did with other Home inhabitants, but somehow I didn't think so. And it didn't really matter. With any luck, we'd escape notice for this one encounter, and I had no illusions about it ever occurring again. We napped for a short time after we made love, and were wakened by irritated static issuing from the now exhausted TV. Gene kissed me sweetly and said, "I gotta go."

"No problem." I smiled.

"All hail, Violet Maris," he said, changing his usual greeting slightly. "You are the bee's knees."

"See you 'round The Home," I said. And he left.

Not as Weird as It Looked

I didn't see Gene anywhere for about a week, though. I casually inquired in the office, pretending to have some official PHAW matters to discuss with him, but Betty said he'd gone up to Boston for some legal business and she wasn't sure when he'd be back. "By next Thursday at the very latest," she called after me. "There's a board meeting that night."

Good, I thought, I won't have to think about all that for a while. I repaired to unit 3, tacked a "writing" note on the door, and settled down with a big pot of tea to try to make some notes for my forthcoming article. I believed this article would be written and published the way you believe you're going to get old and die—barring occasional detours, it's all inevitable, but it just doesn't feel all that real. Still, I did not waver in my devotion to my goal. I was beginning to form a hazy but recognizable picture of the kinds of things I wanted to say about The Home, its culture, and its denizens.

First of all, none of it was as weird as it looked. Sure, it lacked the funding in those days to make refinements, but all the requisite ingredients for a comfortable life were there. No one was really roughing it. The buildings, for the most part, were much nicer inside than out.

A perfect example was the barn, where Bilbo and his family lived, and where he had his studio. I didn't spend much time with them, but I thought it was wonderful. Bilbo's wife, Eileen, an artist herself, had fixed the entire open-concept apartment up to resemble a sort of Moroccan lounge, with tasseled pillows, filmy draperies, and odd bits of furniture painted in brilliant colors. Bilbo and Eileen had three waifish Irish Setters, who draped their shiny, silky, skinny bodies over whatever they could find, looking like bored languishing ladies from Renaissance paintings. Bilbo's studio opened on to the living room, and once while I was there chatting with Eileen, I caught a glimpse of Bilbo and some of the visuals busily sketching a nude male model, who was suspended upside-down on some kind of velveteen-covered structure, with all his manliness flopping about. I have to admit I stared.

"Yeah," Eileen said. "You don't have the opportunity to see too many boys in that exact position, generally speaking." Artistic sophisticates that we were, we giggled.

Secondly, these PHAW fellows were serious. Oh sure, there were a few who weren't *all* that serious, and who would never follow their chosen artistic path any farther than the Sagamore Bridge when their fellowship was over, (and of course, there was me, the one person who absolutely didn't belong), but for the most part, art ruled. The atmosphere was liberating, thrilling even. The fellows were part of something grander than most of us will ever feel. A family? Maybe, for some of them. Some of them formed attachments that would last a lifetime. But I think for most of them it was the feeling, enhanced by the wildness of the location and landscape, that time had stopped for a few months and they could just be who and what they were.

Third, these were The Home's early days, and they were beautifully promising. I had the feeling that in years to come, The Home would make advancements that none of us could even dream of now. Funding and talent would rush in. Knowledge and experience would blossom. There really was no limit to what PHAW could become.

And once I realized that, I also realized that my article wasn't worth writing. Everything about The Home itself was obvious and easily described by any decent journalist. I think what I'd been hoping for was some kind of revelation, but the revelation happened inside me. The only thing that differentiated The Home from the rest of life was the art; otherwise the same things happened there that happened anywhere else. My massive fraud revealed itself to me as what it was: a massive failure of character. I wondered what that meant about Spence, but with everything that was going on with him, I didn't want to stencil any shadows over his good intentions. I think he'd just wanted to help me, and hadn't really thought the rest of it through.

December

Christmas was a-comin' and most of the fellows were going elsewhere for a few days to celebrate with families and friends. I'm not sure any of us realized what Provincetown would be like once all the annoying vestiges of the tourist season were gone. The weather, while not as frigid as it was on the mainland, had a soul-chilling quality that made you feel a bit bipolar—alternately anxious and elated. My own moods, in fact, did vacillate between the two. I was anxious about Spence, I was anxious about my deceitful existence, but I was elated to my core when I stood on the beach at Herring Cove at sunset, one of the rare East Coast places where you could watch the flat golden disk of sun appear to sink into the dark water like a deliciously melting lozenge, with the winter wind whooshing mercilessly around your head. Once someone gave me a tab of LSD and I placed it gingerly under my tongue and drove out there, just gazing at the water for hours. I had intended to continue on to Race Point, but there didn't seem to be any need. Everything was perfect, at least that night.

Gene Pelletier came back into town after his sojourn in Boston, and he and I shared more than a few more nights together. Many, many nights, to be truthful. I'm guessing he must have been more paranoid about being discovered than I was, but he never showed it. I really wanted to tell Jeanette about him, but I didn't. I felt too guilty.

I also felt loved—in a casual way, but it was still satisfying, and, for me, unusual. Gene would show up at the door of unit 3 with a sheaf of papers in a folder and a knapsack that contained such endearing items as a small bouquet of sea lavender and *Rosa rugosa* (the wild Cape rose, believed to have been washed up in shipwrecks many years ago, its fruit rich in vitamins prized by old-time sailors); a bottle of wine, bourbon, or saké; and sometimes a steaming container of Scotch barley soup, a favorite we'd discovered on one of our secret trips to Chatham, when we'd drive down Route 6 in my car to places where the chances of Gene being recognized were slimmer. I don't know what was in that soup, but I do know that I've never tasted anything like it again. Oh yeah, the sheaf of papers that Gene always carried when he visited me was, in case we were noticed, to perpetrate the illusion that I was helping him with his fiction. There was fiction involved, for sure, but it wasn't his writing.

When I'd first encountered Gene in Floaters, way back before I became a fellow, he'd mentioned that he was on the board of The Home and had also been a fellow, but it wasn't until we'd been lovers for a while that I thought to ask him more about it.

"Well, Stella," he said (his pet name for me now), "once upon a time I imagined I was writing the Great American Novel." He grinned. "Boy, was I wrong."

"What do you mean, wrong?"

"I mean I wasn't writing; I was drooling. And it wasn't great or even especially American. At least I had the brains to stop before anyone found out how bad I was. Because I was one of the founders of The Home, they listed me as a fellow in fiction, but it was an honorary title, really. By the second year I made sure I was listed only as a member of the board."

I was intrigued. "You're very self-deprecating, I must say. But you had the impulse to write at some point...what did you write about?"

We were sitting on my unforgiving futon, my head on some pillows and my legs draped over his. Idly, he played with my feet, pulling each toe until I made him stop. "Stella," he said, "I wrote about my crazy life and my crazy wife and all the things that made me the sorry excuse for a man that you see here before you." He got up and poured us two more drinks.

"I'm sorry, Gene," I said. "If you don't want to talk about it, that's okay, really." I had an intense fear of prying too far into his life, since I knew I could never reciprocate properly.

"No, that's okay," he said. "Since you're supposed to be tutoring me on the fine points of fiction, you should know a little bit about it, right?" He laughed, dropping his head back on the wooden futon frame, and went on, in a sort of dreamy voice. I pulled a shawl around me. I felt as if there was going to be a chill, although the glass of saké that Gene had handed me was much warmer than it should have been.

"I met Hannah in college," he began. "She was small and cute and very, very interested in me, God knows why. She reminded me of a young Mary Martin—or maybe that's before your time. *Gamine*, I believe, is the word. Anyway, we hit it off in a sort of general way, although even at the time I felt I was never getting the real Hannah. I found out through the grapevine that her family was loaded—and I do mean loaded—but she never mentioned it to me. After a while we slept together and although she assured me she wasn't a virgin, in my mind I had placed her in that category. Inexperienced, I thought, never thinking that she might just be uninterested." He sighed.

"She really didn't care for sex much," Gene went on. I was getting uncomfortable and wanted to scream out "please stop," but I kept quiet. I had only met Hannah a couple of times and hadn't really formed any strong opinions about her. A couple of people had made snide remarks about her being a bit haughty, but I never thought much about it.

"I mean," Gene went on, "she never really complained, but she never seemed to let go and enjoy herself. I tried to get her to relax, but it only seemed to make her feel hurt and inadequate, so I stopped trying. It kind of hurt my feelings, but I figured that was just who she was. After a while, we just got into a routine. And then she got pregnant."

I'd forgotten about their son Lewis, a lawyer, I think, who lived off-Cape. I'd never met him and Gene didn't talk about him much. I suddenly became acutely aware of the age difference between Gene and me.

"So we got married, and Lewis was born, and little by little she pretty much lost interest in me." Gene sighed. "That's what I wrote about. For a while."

I got up off the futon and went to the window, where furious raindrops had begun pelting the panes. "Wow," I said. "Looks like we're in for a squall."

Gene got up too, and circled his arms around me from behind. "I'm sorry, Stella," he said. "I guess I've maybe said too much—or not enough?"

"Maybe," I said. I turned around. I took his face in my hands and said, "Eugene."

He laughed, and backed up a little. He looked scared.

"Eugene," I said. "I don't know what we're doing, do you? I don't like sneaking around and I bet you don't either. I'm really, really fond of you, but I don't know if this is okay." I hadn't known that I was going to say that, but I was glad I did.

Gene sat down on the futon again, holding on to his ankles. "Right. Of course. I feel the same way. We're just being foolish, and sooner or later people will start talking. And Hannah will find out. I know she won't really care that much—she and I haven't been close in a really long time—but I don't want to hurt her pride. I don't know if you've been wondering, but in case you have: no, I've never done this before—not with anyone at The Home and not with anyone else either. You're the first, my first transgression. You are my star of the sea, old girl, that's all." He looked so genuinely surprised at himself, it crushed my heart.

I went over and sat next to him and let my head fall on his shoulder. "Too much saké," I said. "Let's revisit this in a few days." I kissed him, and he held me for a long time before he left. I wouldn't see Gene again until the big showdown.

Hospiciousness

Spence lay in a hospital bed that had been disguised as a real bed, looking smaller than any adult ever should. He had several angry-looking dark-maroon KS lesions—Kaposi's Sarcoma, a telltale sign of AIDS—on his face, neck, and hands. Ever since that staggering phone call during which Spence described his symptoms and diagnosis, I'd submersed myself in an effort to catch up on the whole subject. I was humbled by the extent of my idiotic head-in-the-sand existence, and horrified, not only by the viciousness of this illness, but by the almost unbelievably cruel insensitivity with which affected populations were being treated. Spencer's illness had taken up prime real estate in my head and colored almost every other emotion I experienced. The weight of it, I knew, was going to bring me to my knees.

The Green Street Residence, a hospice for AIDS patients in Jamaica Plain, made a valiant effort to actually look like a home, but with all the medical paraphernalia the occupants needed, you certainly could never forget where you were. Spence had been at Green Street for almost a month, and they were about to kick him out. It had seemed, when they took him in, that death was imminent, but, against all odds, he'd rallied a bit, and with his doctor's blessing was eager to get back to his apartment. Next to his bed on the little doily-festooned nightstand lay a string of sandalwood mala, Buddhist meditation beads. I picked them up; they were extremely warm. Spence was a devout Buddhist, and I knew he wanted me to join him. He'd given me some pamphlets a while ago. "No pressure," he said. I was looking into it.

It was a gloomy, misty morning, the kind of day when you need the lights on pretty much all the time. "Violet," Spence said, pushing himself up in bed against a mound of starchy pillows, "when do you think I can go home? I'm tired of all this hospiciousness. Has anyone said anything to you? My sister is being very vague. I think she's secretly afraid that I won't have the decency to die any time soon and she'll have to change her return flight to Louisiana. I told her I'm going to have nurses when I get home, but she is determined to stay until I cease to exist."

"Be nice," I said. "You know she means well. She came all the way up here to be with you. I'll take her out to lunch later and see if I can find out what she's thinking."

Spence took my hand, then dropped it. Most people knew that you couldn't contract AIDS through casual contact, but he couldn't let go of the idea that he was disgusting and contagious. He referred to Green Street as "this godforsaken place," and you just had to put up with it. I put up with everything he did and said, in fact, because my soul was blackened by my own transgressions and my heart was splintered by the impending loss of his presence in my life.

Later that morning, Spence's sister, Barbara, dropped by to visit, and seemed delighted to see Spence sitting up in bed and playing poker with me on his tray table. Barb, as she liked to be called, struck me as a sort of socialite wannabe, not rich enough or clever enough to fit in to what she imagined the upper class to be, but well-meaning and interesting in her own gently flamboyant way. Her primly shellacked French-twisted hair looked as if it would have been lovely if set free. We exchanged greetings, shook hands, and made plans to meet for lunch at a local bistro. She didn't seem to mind that I looked a wreck, and I liked that. I left her with Spence and ran off to do a million errands, both Spence's and mine.

Barbara Bayrose was late for lunch. I didn't really mind; it gave me a chance to absorb the unique character of the place, an old-fashioned family restaurant with a sparsely stocked bar and baskets of shiny, knobby rolls on the tables. I considered the idea that the rolls were plastic, or maybe varnished papier-mâché. There was a genuine daisy in a vase, however, and the atmosphere was comfortable and clean. Barbara made quite an entrance, flouncing down in a chair with a couple of shopping bags, her immense purse, and a sort of wooly boa dripping from her camel-hair coat.

"Oh, Violet," she puffed, "I'm so sorry. I should have taken a cab, but I thought I knew the T well enough to get here on time. Unfortunately, it dropped me off about six blocks from here and I had to hoof it." She seemed quite peeved. It occurred to me that she thought the trolley was at fault for neglecting to drop her off closer to her destination.

"No big deal," I said, and smiled. This was, after all, Spence's only sibling. I decided to love her.

Barb was already wading deep into the menu and waving her hand with comic imperiousness to attract attention. The only waitperson, it seemed, was also the bartender, a stout gentleman with center-parted hair, and when he saw Barb's hand circling about over our heads, he dropped whatever he was doing behind the bar and ran right over. Poor man.

I'll spare you the details of Barb's elaborate ordering system. She took it upon herself to order for me too, and out of pity for our server and an extreme case of bafflement, I did not object. Suffice it to say that we ended up with shrimp cocktails, beer, a huge plate of salad (to share), and cheeseburgers. I don't think she even wanted a cheeseburger, but she couldn't find anything she did want. And I certainly didn't want one; I don't eat meat, so I wasn't too happy. When our food arrived, I slid the burger out of the bun, scraped some cheese onto one of the knobby rolls from the basket, added some of the salad, and had myself a fine old time. Barb had not stopped talking for a minute. I was on my second beer when I suddenly tuned in to what she was saying. Everything I'd just eaten began to march noisily around my innards as if a war were going on between what I should have eaten and what I'd subjected myself to.

"So, Violet," Barb went on, "will you do us the honor of serving as editor for this project? I haven't talked to Spence about it yet, of course, but I know you'd be his first choice." She was arranging the stiff, papery shrimp tails artistically along the edge of her plate. Over her head, I could see our bewildered server observing us intently while drying some water glasses with a striped towel. All that's needed here, I thought, is a barbershop quartet.

I was terrified. While I'd been woolgathering, Barb had been describing to me how, as she was straightening up Spence's apartment and tending to poor Dusty, she'd discovered some interesting papers spread out on her brother's desk. They were copies of his stories—probably on their way to me. I tried to pick up my beer, but the glass was too hot to hold.

"Wow, Barb," I said. "thank you so much for thinking of me, but I'll need some time to consider it, you know? Could you wait a bit for an answer?" I didn't want to be specific, hoping to hold her off as long as possible. "And maybe not talk to Spence yet?" I said. "I think he's got enough on his mind."

I smiled what I hoped was a doleful smile.

"Of course," Barb said, folding her napkin into a neat rectangle. "That's fine. You think about it and we'll wait to talk to Spence until he's back in his apartment again. Oh, and, Violet, I'm not getting along all that well with poor Dusty. I think she really misses Spence."

I was somewhat relieved. "Don't worry about Dusty," I said. "She'll come around. Try buying her love with catnip. I think Spence has some hidden on the top shelf in the pantry."

"Wonderful!"

And we parted. I noticed gratefully that Barbara had left an enormous tip for our poor bartender.

The next morning a patient transport van brought Spence back to his apartment, Barbara settled him in, and I returned to The Home. My head was splitting and the steering wheel of my little Citation was as warm as a magazine left too long in the sun.

WHY WE'D NEED A BIG SEDAN

Cordelia Hight was standing on the curb near the bus station at 7:30 a.m. when I walked down to Buoy-O-Buoy's for my coffee and oat cakes. She looked only casually costumed, unlike her preposterous everyday self, but over her curls she did sport a crimson velvet cloche that looked like it might have belonged to Garbo.

She waved at me, and I crossed the street to talk to her, which, generally, I had no idea how to do. I didn't dislike Cordelia; I just always felt a little flustered around her. I'd heard from a couple of people that her poetry was pretty good, though. I also knew she was the designated gossip for our cohort at The Home—all news started with Cordelia. By the time news trickled down to me, however, it was usually very old.

"Where ya' going?" I smiled at her. "I mean if you don't mind my asking. I like your hat."

She smiled back, preciously. I wondered if it was exhausting to compose one's face into such theatrical expressions all the time, or if it came naturally to her.

"Just down to Hyannis to the dentist," she said. "I seem to have chipped a tooth on that ridiculous rock candy they sell along the pier."

"Ouch. Sorry."

"No bother," she said. "I must say I enjoy a little excursion now and again. Maybe I'll go to the movies after my appointment." Her face lit up, as if she'd just thought of something incredibly brilliant.

"I think *Witness* is showing now. Do you like Harrison Ford?"

"Oh, he's diviiine," she sighed, making a little swoony motion with her head and shoulders as if Harrison himself had been standing there. She gave me a piercing look. "What I really love is that drive-in theater in Wellfleet. We should all find someone with a really big car and make an event of it sometime."

I had no idea who "we" was supposed to be, but I played along. This was getting interesting. I knew Cordelia slept around, but I didn't know who she was favoring lately. "That sounds like fun," I said.

I saw Cordelia's bus rounding the corner and heading for the stop. Suddenly her whole demeanor changed into something less innocent and charming. Her eyes narrowed and she stared into mine. "Yeeees," she said. "That would be fun. We'll definitely need a big sedan—not anything as uncomfortable as a Land Rover."

I couldn't speak. The bus pulled up and Cordelia wrangled her long skirts up the steps, calling "Bye, honey," over her shoulder at me.

I didn't go to breakfast.

GETTING ALL FORMAL

I walked up and down Commercial Street and then back to The Home, but didn't see Gene's car anywhere. Usually he was easy to find, but not today. So I called him both at home and at his real estate office. No answer at his home, but he picked up at the office.

"Violet of the Sea!" he said. "How are you?" We hadn't communicated since that last night at unit 3.

"I'm sorry, Gene," I blurted out. "I just ran into Cordelia. She made a point of letting me know that you and I are an item in her gossip book. I just thought you should know." I held my breath. I felt as if I had tossed a large stone into the still lake that was usually Gene, but there was not a ripple.

"Oh, okay, kiddo," he said. "I'm not surprised, are you? I mean, it's kind of hard to keep this kind of thing secret at The Home."

I was relieved he wasn't freaking out, but I still had questions. "But what about Hannah?"

"I doubt she'll hear about it," he said. "She's not really in the loop around town. And even if she does, she'll never mention it to me unless she wants to use it against me somehow."

"Oh," I said. "That's sad."

"I know," he said. And then, "I miss you, Stella. Are we ready to talk yet? I have some ideas…" He actually sounded a little hopeful.

The sound of his voice was killing me. I suddenly realized, that without having given myself any kind of permission to do so, I had fallen hard for Gene. I loved the way his body inhabited the space in my apartment, the air around him displaced by his essence, invisibly fanning out around him in waves of simplicity and comfort. Gene was a person who could just *be*. All I needed was to touch any part of his body with any part of mine to find a deep, instant healing—the kind I'd forgotten it was possible to experience. The sex was great, but it wasn't the main course. Gene had a profound warmth of spirit and a big, comfortable body to go with it. These were things I'd never had. He was stuck fast in my heart. I had to admit it. A guy who deserved better than my miserable, fraudulent self. Nice work, Violet.

"I miss you too," I said, "but, no, not quite yet, okay? I think I'll be going up to Boston for a few days next week to visit Spence. Maybe when I come back."

"Let me know," he said with a bit of a catch in his voice. "And if you need help with anything—anything at all—while you're in Boston, leave a message for me here. I check every day, even if I don't come in. And I'm happy to help, you know that." As always, he was relentlessly decent.

"I know, Eugene."

He chuckled. "It turns me on when you get all formal."

PAX VOBISCUM

Jeanette and Phrank invited me to her place for dinner. I was happy to hear that Christine would be out that night, since I was finding it harder and harder to avoid her polite and intelligent questions about "my" work. I was looking forward to seeing my two friends and relaxing a bit. My brain was churning with thoughts of Spence and Gene. It felt as if there were a giant wheel of fortune in my head, and whenever I set it spinning, another scary prize clicked in.

I brought an offering of bread and wine. Phrank opened the door and received it solemnly, sacramentally. "Pax vobiscum," he said, and kissed me on the cheek. We shared a history of Catholic schools. Jeanette was less clerical, crunching me in a huge hug and jumping up and down. "Oh, *finally* we get to see you." She grinned. "Come on in."

Dinner was delicious—fresh flounder and little round potatoes that made me think how Spence would have liked them. Unit 10 had a fireplace with a big old flowered sofa in front of it, and after we watched Phrank struggle to light newspapers and damp kindling, we all sat back and gazed dreamily into the flames. It was the first night in a while that I hadn't felt like a nervous wreck. I should seek out friends more, I thought, then remembered why I shouldn't.

Conversation drifted all about, then settled on the inevitable Home talk: what we were working on. Phrank said he was stuck; he couldn't write his way out of a snare he'd written himself into. Jeanette said she was working, but she wasn't sure where it was going. That was the sort of thing most poets said about their work, I thought to myself. I just didn't get it. But the bigger picture was that she was struggling to complete her first full-length collection of poems, hoping to have it ready to submit to publishers by the time her fellowship was over. We offered her words of support.

"What about you, Violet?" Phrank asked. Tiny Jeanette was by this time curled up in his lap like a cat, and they looked ridiculously cute. "Anything new?"

I was ready. "Not really new," I said, "but I've decided to rework some really old stuff I found. I've been working on these stories a long time, you know." I was still amazed at the facility with which I could spew forth outright lies. All feelings of relaxation began to fall away like stylish clothes I'd borrowed but had to return.

"Hmm," said Phrank. I saw Jeanette surreptitiously poke him in the ribs.

"Hmm?" I said, trying to make a joke of it.

"Oh, nothing. I was just thinking. Violet, I'll never get over how expertly you pull off writing in the voice of someone so totally unlike yourself who lives in a place so totally unlike where you're from. It's a gift."

He sounded sincere, but I couldn't be sure. "Why thank you," I said. "Really. Thanks." I hoped that would be the end of it.

"And also," Phrank went on, "it amazes me just how *many* of these stories you produce. I mean, most of us can't crank out more than a few pages a day if we're lucky." He was starting to sound a little hostile.

Jeanette fairly bounded off Phrank's lap, picked up the wine bottle on the coffee table, and refilled all our glasses. She handed mine to me.

I dropped it. It was too hot.

"Oh God, I'm sorry!" I leaped up and started for the kitchen to fetch a towel.

"Don't worry about it," Jeanette said, laughing. "These old boards are used to all kinds of spills, I'm sure."

It broke the evil spell, at least for the time being. The three of us chatted some more, and then Phrank said Cordelia had told him that she was planning a PHAW night out at the Wellfleet drive-in. I was sweating through my blouse so much I feared someone would comment on it.

"And she said we'd have to look around for people with big sedans." He grinned at me. "Chevy Citations need not apply," he said. "No Land Rovers either."

I gave up. I gave in. "Look, you guys," I said. "I take

it you know about me and…the Land Rover." I tried to giggle, but some other creepy noise came out. I paused, and a slow drop of perspiration dribbled down my forehead. "I don't know if it's still anything, actually."

Jeanette smacked Phrank on the arm. "Why'd you have to bring that up?" she said. Phrank was slumped over, obviously drunk.

She moved over to me and put her arm around my shoulders. "Don't worry, honey. We're not going to tell."

Phrank sat up again, laughing. "Well, we don't have to, do we?" he said. "Everybody knows." Then he looked directly at me. "I guess your 'no hanky-panky' policy was rescinded, eh, Violet?" Phrank gave me a sarcastic little wave, tottered off into the bedroom, and pretty much slammed the door.

I gathered up my jacket and bag while Jeanette fussed around me in a flurry of radical dismay. "It's okay, Jeanette, no hard feelings. Maybe I can talk to you about this with you privately some time, okay?" I gave her a quick hug. "Thanks for, uh, a great meal."

Om

By the time I'd walked the short distance from unit 10 to unit 3, I was shaking with fear and sadness. I decided I needed to keep busy and set about packing up a few things to take on my trip to Boston the next day, but after a few minutes I just sat down on the futon and cried. First Cordelia and now this. And I was disappointed in Phrank, whom I'd believed to be a good guy. But he *is* a good guy, I admonished myself; he's good to Jeanette and her mom, and he tried to be nice to you, you insufferable, self-centered jerk. You're the one who damaged his spirit, if not his heart. I was just pulling myself together when there was a knock at the door. An assistant from the office had an urgent message for me: please call Barbara.

Spence was suddenly much worse. I could meet Barb at the hospice and say my goodbyes if I got there in time. Without even grabbing my half-packed bag, I sprang for my car, and I broke every speed limit on my way back to Boston. When I got there, Spence was still with us.

But he looked gaunt and ethereal. There was a faint odd fragrance in the room, like some kind of old-timey men's cologne, not unpleasant, just unnerving. I thought it might be my soul melting. Barb said Spence was on serious pain meds, so I shouldn't expect too much, but I could tell he knew I was there. I kissed his forehead, which was warm and papery. "Come out in the hall a minute, will you?" Barb said.

Out in the hallway, she told me, "Spence gave me a message for you. Last night, just before the drugs put him to sleep, he pulled me down to his face and whispered, 'Tell Violet I love her, okay, Barb? I always meant to, but I never told her,' and I said I would." She hugged me.

I collapsed into some kind of bamboo armchair and Barb handed me one of the zillion boxes of tissues that littered the entire building. So much crying and blowing of noses. We cried, and blew our noses. Eventually, we went back into the room.

What greeted us was a beautiful scene. While we'd been weeping in the hallway, four of Spence's Buddhist friends had arrived, and were standing next to his bed quietly chanting. Barb had told me they were coming, but I guess I expected monks or nuns in saffron robes. These were just ordinary-looking people: a middle-aged couple, an older gentleman, and a younger woman. They had laced the string of mala beads through Spence's fingers, and, although he still appeared to be sleeping, he looked more peaceful, less pained. Barb and I crept back out to the hallway, where, with Spence's door open now, we could still hear the chime-like cadences of their voices, punctuated by "ooooms."

"Violet," Barb said, "I'm so disappointed in Spence's colleagues and friends. You know he was very popular all his life, and very kind to everyone, but although I called a number of people in his address book, only you and Larry Antiger have shown any interest in seeing him." She sighed deeply.

"I'm not that surprised," I said. "People are afraid to visit here, even though they know better. But it is, I agree, dispiriting."

"And who's Larry Antiger?" I added.

"I'd never met him before, Violet, and if you don't know who he is, I'm only guessing that they might have shared a relationship at some point. He's about Spence's age, professional looking and kind, and he spent quite a while in Spence's room. I heard them laughing just before he left. I was going to ask Spence, but when I went back into the room, he had a look on his face that I did not recognize, and I said to myself, 'Barb, you old busybody, let your poor brother have some privacy.'" She laughed. "Can you believe it? I'm trying to behave!"

Suddenly a little red light started blinking above Spence's door, two nurses ran in, and the Buddhists filed quickly out. We started to rush to his bedside, but then realized we needed to let the nurses do whatever they were doing. They didn't do much. One of them walked past us, patting Barb on the arm, and the other came up to us and took one of each of our hands in hers. "He's almost gone," she said, "but if you go right in I believe he just might still be able to hear you."

Spence died about five minutes later. Barbara smoothed what was left of his hair back and I picked up the extremely warm mala beads, which had fallen to the side of his bed, and dropped them into my pocket. Spence would always be with me, as would the weight of all the other souls who had fallen to this disease, a disease that would shatter so many lives and shame so many others who had no compassion.

Barb and I had no more tears left. We went back to Spence's apartment and drank too much bourbon. Dusty seemed to know, shunned our attentions, and disappeared to sleep by herself on Spence's bed.

In the morning, Barb left to take care of details before returning to Baton Rouge, after assuring me that I should stay in the apartment as long as I wanted. I said I might actually want to take over the lease at some point, and she seemed open to that. And of course I promised that Dusty would always have a home with me. I didn't want to take her back to Provincetown, though, so I arranged that the kindly downstairs neighbors would care for her until I could return. It would be better for Dusty to stay in her familiar home, and they seemed delighted to take on the job.

HALFWAY THERE

About halfway back to The Home, I stopped to call Gene. I was feeling fragile and slow, and before I could even tell him my sad news, he blurted out, "Hannah's left me!"

I was stunned. Too much was happening.

"What?" I said. I could barely get that one word out.

"It's so crazy, Stella. While we were having breakfast yesterday morning, I noticed she had already applied a lot of makeup—unusual for her—and was wearing a classy pantsuit, not the kind of thing one wears for hanging around Ptown. I asked her what was up. She was almost serene. She said, 'I'm leaving you, Gene. First I'm going to my sister's in Wareham, and after that I don't know, but I'll be in touch.' Then she got up, cleared the dishes and walked calmly out of the room.

"I followed her. As she was tossing the last few things into a small suitcase, she said, 'Look, Gene. We're not in love anymore. You know it and I know it. I want more than this. I don't love this town the way you do. I'm not hip and I'm not artsy and I don't like fish. I don't hate you; I just want to get away from you.' Then she turned around and faced me, with tears in her eyes, and we hugged, and I said, 'Let me know if I can help in any way,' or something lame like that. And then she left by the front door, jumped into her Camry, and drove off." Gene paused and cleared his throat, clearly stricken by his own matter-of-fact rendition of the scene.

"Good grief," was all I could think of. And then, "I'm sorry."

"Don't be. It's all for the best. It was a shock, though. I guess I always thought I'd be the one to go first—especially after I met you."

I sighed. "Wow," I said, idiotically. "That is really something."

"But *you* called me," Gene said. "Are you on your way home? How did it go? How is Spence?"

"I'm halfway there," I said. "Can we meet up later today? Maybe around dinner time?"

"Sure," he said. "I'll pick up some of our soup and meet you at your place around seven?" And then, as an afterthought, "Geez, I guess now you could actually come to my house, but—"

"No, no," I said. "It's too soon. See you at seven in unit 3."

In the Breakdown Lane

I knew Gene would be on time—he always was— and just before seven o'clock I started feeling really sick to my stomach. My head hurt. I was shaky and sweaty and I seriously considered the idea that I was going to pass out. Great, I thought, Gene will knock, receive no answer, and he'll go get a key from the office and find me slumped over on the floor like a damp old doll. I washed my face and tried to pull myself together. I was losing it. Spence's death was starting to hit me hard, grinding away at all the things that usually held me together, and then there was the Hannah story. What the hell. What impeccable timing. Usually, I was a person who expected that things would eventually get better, but I didn't feel that way this time. I felt as if the universe was instructing me to change before it was too late, but I didn't know how. Maybe it was too late already.

I fell onto Gene's chest as soon as he came through the door. He dropped the bag of takeout he was carrying and just held me tight. "Oh Jesus," he said. "Did Spence die?"

When I was able to stop sobbing, I told him the whole story.

The whole story.

I went to the kitchen cupboard. When I'd moved in, I noticed someone had left half a pack of Marlboros on the top shelf. I lit one up. It had been years since I'd smoked, but I didn't even cough. Gene stared at me. He took a handkerchief from his pocket and wiped his brow. He was sitting on the edge of my bed, and I joined him, trying to blow the smoke from my cigarette away from his face. And then I slowly moved back from him. I felt merciless and calm. "Gene," I said, "you know…my stories…"

"Sure," he said, puzzled. "What about them?"

"Spence wrote them," I said. I moved back another few inches on the bed and looked at Gene.

"Spence wrote them, and I've been pretending they're mine."

He got up and went to the window, looking out, with his back to me.

"No," he said.

"I have to tell you the whole story," I said, but he was already putting his jacket on. He never turned around to look at me. He closed the door behind him very quietly.

I watched the Land Rover speed out of the parking lot.

I started wildly stuffing things into bags and boxes—whatever I could find—and filling up my car with all my pitiful belongings. By this time, it was close to eight, and getting dark, so I didn't attract much notice. I saw Cordelia's face at her window as I passed by, but I didn't care. I had to get out of there fast.

I didn't know how long it would take Gene to turn me in, but of course he would have to: he was the board chair. I didn't care what my punishment would be, but I knew I could not stay in town for one more second and be forced to have conversations with anyone about any of this. They could arrest me if that's what they wanted to do. I actually had no idea what they'd want to do. It didn't matter. By eight-thirty I was on the road to Boston again.

I went directly to Spence's and was welcomed by a confused and love-starved Dusty. She stuck close to me all that evening, and I was grateful. Her softness and neediness were almost overpowered by my own insanities, but enough of it got through that I fell into a crazy, troubled sleep.

ASHES TO ASHES

Five months passed. I didn't get arrested. It appeared that The Home's board did not spread the word of my shame, which I suppose would have cast aspersions on them as well, for not foreseeing such an evil possibility. I hope they revised their entry applications to include a declaration of artistic ownership. I got a letter from a lawyer representing The Home about a week after I left town, demanding that I repay the stipend I'd received and sign a document saying that I would never publish a story about my experience there. I did both things. I had been intending to repay the money anyway of course, but I'd had to wait until Spence's bequest to me came through. After I paid The Home, I had enough to live on for about a year. Without that, I'm not sure what I would have done. Spence had saved me. I'd lost all caring about myself and my situation. I considered therapy, but I didn't know where to start. And I would have to find a job someday, and reenter civilization, I guess. Make friends? How would I do that? I just had no idea how to tackle a future. I had no idea what my penance should be, or even how to find out. I never again heard from any of the other residents at PHAW, not even Jeanette. I've heard that, according to maritime law, you can keep anything you recover from a bonafide shipwreck; I wondered if there'd be anything to recover from this one.

I had taken on Spence's lease, and lived in his gorgeous, mostly furnished apartment in total isolation with Dusty. Barbara had wanted only a few of his possessions. I missed everything about Provincetown, especially walking the sandy woodland paths, the careless skies peppered with soaring gulls, and most of all the sea, but I knew I could never go back there. The only thing I did that was even remotely healthy was to walk around nearby Jamaica Pond, about a mile and a quarter in circumference, I think, a few times a week. Barb had arranged a lovely memorial for Spence in Louisiana, with lots of flowers and no speeches, but I couldn't bring myself to go. She told me she'd scattered his ashes in a lake near their childhood home. Barb mentioned my editing Spence's stories once or twice more, but then I guess she became distracted, thank heaven. Eventually, we lost touch.

I was on one of my walks one day when, along the back perimeter of the pond where people could park, I saw—or thought I saw—an old Land Rover drive by. I walked faster, terrified to see who was driving. The chances of it having been Gene's car were, I told myself, miniscule. Still, I was scared. I'd thought about Gene a lot, needless to say. Betraying his trust in me was even worse in a way than lying to get accepted to The Home. He was a decent, kind, affectionate person and I had come to love him. I was a lying, selfish bitch. That was all there was to it.

A week later I was coming out of the grocery store when I saw the car again. This time, it was parked at the far end of the lot, and before I could get a good look at it, it backed out of its space and sped off. I couldn't see the driver, or the license plate, or anything. How could there be so many of these cars around here, I asked myself. I couldn't remember ever noticing them in the past. I walked home, perplexed.

The next morning, after lying around in bed with Dusty for a while, I threw a sweater over my long johns, fed Dusty, and revved up the coffeemaker. Outside, clearly visible from the kitchen window, an old blue-grey Land Rover was trying to crush itself into a ridiculously tight parking spot across the street. It succeeded. My entire body went cold. I ran to the utility drawer, where I remembered Spence had once kept a pair of binoculars for watching his beloved wrens. The binoculars were still there. They were almost too warm to hold.

By this time, the car had squeezed into its chosen space, its proximity to the car behind it obscuring the plate, but with the aid of Spence's binoculars, I could make out a permit sticker on the rear window: Cape Cod National Seashore Park. I laid the binoculars back in the drawer, picked up Dusty, and hugged her very tightly to my chest.

"You be sweet to him, Dusty," I whispered in her ear, "no matter what he has to say to me. You just be sweet."

ACKNOWLEDGEMENTS

Enormous love and gratitude to:

My husband, Carey Reid, who somehow always believes.

My brother, Robert Early James Wald, who says, "Yes, I want to read it," whenever I ask.

All my friends, loved ones, and ghosts from those long-ago days in Provincetown, three stunning years that have enriched my life for decades.

My dear friend Ellen Wittlinger, who has left this earth. El, how dare you leave so soon. You would have had fun with this book.

My dear friend Garth Pitman, who fought AIDS with the courage of an archangel. I miss you.

The Fine Arts Work Center in Provincetown. My two fellowships, so many years ago, led to a third fascinating year in that magical town. Without all that, this book could not have been born. I've got sand in my shoes forever.